# THUNDER 'N' TURF

## THE REGENCY ADVENTURES OF KATHERINE PENELOPE LUCAS

PAM TURNBULL

TAU PRESS LTD

Thunder 'n' Turf by Pam Turnbull.

Copyright © 2018 Pam Turnbull. All rights reserved.

ISBN 978-1-910342-94-7



Published by Tau Press Ltd.

Cover by Jane Dixon-Smith (jdsmith-design.com).

❋ Created with Vellum

Pip pressed his nose against the window of the carriage as they passed into Epsom. He had never seen so many people and in so many different colours and styles. Standing apart was a man in a bright red waistcoat – this is what Pip had wanted to see: the Robin Redbreasts. A double-breasted coat with slightly tarnished gilt buttons (Uncle Thomas would not approve), a leather stock, white gloves, tall black leather hat, top boots and the essential scarlet waistcoat. It was cold, so the cloak probably covered the pistol and heavy sabre but he knew there would be a truncheon and a pair of handcuffs at hand and ready to use.

Uncle Thomas had told him all about the Bow Street Runners and had once met their founder John Townsend. The stories were exciting, dangerous and exotic when you were six. At the exalted aged of nine he was still smitten. As he began to lower the window to see one last glimpse of his hero, he knocked his sister's arm.

"Don't you dare open that window until we are out of the town, Philip Bartholomew Bentley. It's noisy, smelly and cold!"

"It won't be any warmer in the countryside!"

The soothing tones of Miss Lucas interrupted, "I wonder why there are so many people here? Can you see anything, children?"

At that three sets of eyes scanned their surroundings.

"A balloon, a balloon… Oh please Miss Lucas can we stop, can we?"

At 14, Sarah was trying hard to leave the schoolroom, but faced by a balloon her child's love of novelty persisted. Where her brother was fascinated by crime, she was bewitched by the idea of adventure, which the colours of the balloon promised. Seeing an opportunity to explore and perhaps even meet his hero, Pip joined in.

Miss Lucas knew that she should be strong on this point. Her instructions were clear; deliver the children to their grandmother for Easter and then return them to their educational establishments in Bath. Not that difficult, but a distinct change for someone used to running her father's life and mediating disputes between the ladies in his life. But she was not that much older than Sarah and also wanted to see the balloon.

It took about five minutes before Kitty Lucas realised she was out of her depth. The coachman had arranged to meet them by the church. They could see the tower from the balloon grounds, so what could possibly go wrong?

To begin with neither child saw it as imperative or even necessary for them to stay close to her. As they both dashed off in opposite directions, she paused to consider which one she should chase after first, and in that pause they were both lost in the milling crowd.

Whether it was blind panic, natural common sense or sheer dumb luck, Kitty followed the surge of humanity towards the balloon. Thankfully, someone with a commercial bent had erected a fence and the main field could only be accessed via a rough table and the donation of two pennies. As she knew Sally's pin money lay in her reticule, she began to breathe easier.

However, her eldest charge was not to be thwarted by lack of funds. She caught sight of Sally at the same time as Sally ingeniously added herself to a large family party. Waved through by the man at the table, she was now approaching the balloon.

The envelope was becoming larger and more stable as the air made its way inside. The orange, yellow and red of the strips of cloth glowed in the sunlight, given extra depth and hue by the furnace below them. As she got closer, the roar became more noticeable and the balloon took on the persona of an animal on a leash. Fanciful she knew, and in other circumstances she could and would have enjoyed the sight. Just not at this moment!

Anxious as she was not to lose sight of the girl, she lost her place in the queue to a large lady in purple. Despite her concerns, she was intrigued by the quantity of purple one person could wear and in such a profusion – pleats, layers, tucks, gathers, as well as a matching hat which was probably the ugliest thing she had ever seen - especially when she could swear she saw a blackbird (stuffed) roosting in its innards. Unbidden came a greater insight, the slight rip in the lace made good by a clumsy hand, extra tucks made by the same seamstress, chapped wrists and a musty smell. All painted the picture for Kitty of a washerwoman whose apparel was probably the result of an unpaid debt and originally made for someone of wider girth. There was a story or intrigue here, but not one for her.

She paid her entrance fee and re-focussed on the spot

where she had last seen Sally. Momentary panic ensued before she finally spotted her walking towards the pilots.

"No, no, oh please no," she muttered to herself as she made her way over the uneven ground. As the field was one which usually housed cattle, there were the inevitable obstacles in her way which made her grateful she was wearing her sensible boots, but even still she held her skirts a little higher than usual. After all, she did not have a maid to clean up after her, or a doting guardian to buy her new ones. A wave of resentment and self-pity swept over her as she regarded her charge standing gazing in honest admiration at the men positioning the basket. Sally had never had to manage or make do and mend and she would never have to. But Kitty was not built for envy and Sally's shining eyes dispelled her bad humour.

"Sally, never run off like that! I might never have found you," she exclaimed as she hugged the young girl around the shoulders.

"Oh, Miss Lucas, isn't it quite wonderful. They take passengers, you know. Do you think…"

"No, Sally, I do not. Whatever would your grandmother say? Now let us find your brother so he does not miss the start."

There was now a steady stream of people coming through the gate. The hedgerow seemed thinner to the left of it, so with Sally firmly clasped in one hand they set off. At this time of year foliage was limited but the hawthorn and brambles retained their barbs and as Kitty tried to make her way through the fence she was soon well and truly snagged. Trying to keep composure and dignity in such a situation is not made easier when one's young friend is clutching her side and swaying to her peals of laughter.

"I am sure it is very funny, Sally, but do something. Pass me that stick."

"Oh, Miss Lucas I haven't laughed so much for an age. Miss

Pettigrew says laughing is vulgar, but it does make you feel so much better."

"I agree," echoed a new voice from behind Kitty. It sounded amused, the accent educated and the tone sardonic. Unfortunately, her predicament prevented her from moving to see the owner. Male obviously, and Sally's well executed curtsey told its own story.

A couple of slashes with a stick and Kitty was free. A moment later, both ladies where on the desired side of the fence.

"You know, I encourage my tenants to put in gates so that this does not happen. The brambles are to catch calves not petticoats!"

Kitty forced herself to look into her rescuer's face. She predicted that she not only looked a mess, but that she was blushing in a most unbecoming way. As she opened her mouth to explain, Sally piped up:

"Our apologies, sir, for any damage done. If you would advise me of the amount, I will ensure that you are reimbursed. We were in a hurry as my little brother has wandered off, and..."

Sally's very expensive education had come to her rescue but her lack of experience let her down at the end. The appearance of their rescuer was her undoing, Sally knew very little about men's fashions and, to be frank, she knew very little about women's, relying on grandmother to order what was required, but she knew that this gentleman's clothes were something which neither her grandfather or Uncle Thomas would wear. And the colour ...

Miss Lucas's knowledge came from her very particular friend, Miss Trevor whose letters were full of entertaining anecdotes and descriptions of the the very best society, or the Ton as it was commonly known. She had thought them exaggerations to entertain a friend, now she saw that they were a true and accurate description. The boots caught her attention initially. They shone like glass and fitted perfectly the legs in front of her. The yellow trousers were very different - fitted, with no hint of the breeches her father always wore. The jacket was a glorious blue and the necktie was a work of art. She knew these had names like the Waterfall and that they were the height of fashion. Luckily, this one was not as elaborate as some Jane had described, but it was more than enough for a field in the middle of April.

There was probably a hat, but Kitty's attention was riveted on the man's face. He had the bluest eyes she had ever seen and they were laughing. A shout from behind him killed the laughter and a bored, languid expression took residence, bowing slightly he left to join a party of similarly attired men.

"Clarky, they're here!"

Looking up they saw Pip pulling a man in a cloak and red waistcoat in their direction.

"Turn around, sis, you'll miss it."

As one, they turned to see the balloon tugging against its mooring ropes as men and women were helped aboard the basket. The steps were removed and all but one of the ropes released. The final rope was longer and allowed the balloon to ascend. The three watched in amazement as the rope was then hauled away by a cart horse and the balloon descended to applause. As its passengers alighted with varying amounts of aplomb, others eagerly exchanged coins for the experience.

The clambering of the crowd brought Kitty to her senses and she turned to her two charges. Both transfixed by the balloon, she brought her gaze to Pip's companion.

"Thank you, sir for returning the boy, I hope he was no trouble."

"None at all, miss, though I don't know why he thought I was a Runner."

And with that he doffed he cap and returned the way he had

come past the party of richly clad men which included her rescuer. They had now been joined by some equally elegantly dressed ladies,. She was about to turn back to the balloon when she caught sight of something pass between her rescuer's left hand and Pip's Runner

"Come on, we better make our way to the church."

The rest of the journey was relatively unremarkable. Although there was a little business with some ducks as they were leaving the town. The silly creatures dashed across the road, and Sarah was convinced they had hit one. She insisted they stop the coach, and would only consent to continue after she had checked the wheel, tracked down the ducks on the adjacent pond, and assured herself none were hurt. Kitty hoped duck was not on tonight's menu.

A striking church bell drew everyone's attention to the time and soon they were bounding along at a fair speed. The road was straight and even, and the movement of the carriage began to lull everyone into a state of mild torpor. Kitty began to relax.

The short spring day was drawing to a close when their destination came into view. Bare trees accompanied them down the drive masking a small park on either side. Soon lights began to pop out from between the branches as the windows of the house came closer while a beam of light issued from the opening door as the carriage swung into position. All was excitement as steps were lowered, feet ran to welcoming relatives and bodies unloaded boxes and cases. But amidst all this homecoming Miss Lucas stood alone and somewhat in the way.

"This way, miss, Catherine will show you the way." And with an authoritative beckoning finger Catherine took up Kitty's bags and preceded her through the main door.

After half an hour of sitting alone in a pleasant but functional room, Kitty confirmed that her decision to be a companion, rather than a governess, was probably the right one. She was not family or a guest, so she couldn't avail herself of the house. She was not a servant as such so could not pass the door to the servant's quarters. "Neither fish nor fowl nor good red meat," she muttered to herself. Yet knowing what you couldn't do didn't help when you wanted something to eat. Should she ring or just go wandering. As there was no obvious bell-pull, her options were limited to one. Straightening her dress and hair, she pinned on what she hoped was a confident expression and opened the door.

Her bedroom was situated next to a darkened room which light from the corridor traced the tell-tale signs of a nursery. Dust covers and a coldness in the air seemed to indicate that it had not seen use in some time. Along the corridor were children's rooms, and three of these were in use as fires blazed in the small grates, a cousin for Pip and Sally perhaps? One door remained. It too opened into darkness, but here the outlines suggested a schoolroom. Returning quickly to her room for a candle, she lit the sconces and took a good look. Here was somewhere she could legitimately explore. No expense had been spared, there were primers in Latin and Greek and good quality paper and pens rather than slates she was used to. There was even a chalking space on the wall with a large nautical map pinned next to it.

"I was always very fond of maps," said a voice from the door. Suppressing an unladylike yelp, she turned to face a pair of very blue eyes and a look of recognition.

"Miss Lucas, our hostess was enquiring after you and I volunteered to find you as she was being entertained in some detail by her grandchildren's experiences with ducks and balloons."

"You have the advantage of my name, but ..."

"I apologise." And with a slight incline of the head. "Edward Gregory at your service."

"Children are not to your liking then?" she replied rising from a suitable curtsy.

"When I have some of my own I am sure I will find them delightful. Shall we?"

And thus it was, a short time later, that Kitty entered the drawing room of The Towers on the arm of Edward Gregory, a handsome man who made it his business to rescue governesses and their charges from brambles in cow fields. Delivered to an elegantly quaffed lady, she made her curtsy.

"Ahh, Miss Lucas. Thank you for bringing my doves home. As the children are dining with us tonight, I asked Tipping to set a place for you." And with a wave of a hand Kitty was dismissed into the corner, where a scowling boy sat holding a book.

Pip and Sally were petted and championed by their grandmother, Lady Constance, while their grandfather, Mr Fitzgerald, held court at the other end of the table. Apart from the blue-eyed Mr Gregory the names of the others at the table had passed her by. She guessed that one was a local landowner, another a member of the clergy but the others deigned neither to look in her direction nor try to engage her in conversation, so she repaid the compliment. Her scowling companion she discovered was called Claudius and was being prepared for Oxford by the local curate Mr Bostock who, for his pains, had been invited to dine.

From the other end of the table Lady Constance issued a constant stream of instructions to the fifteen-year-old boy.

"Don't let Claudius have any red meat, Miss Lucas, his constitution is not strong."

"Claudius, little sips of boiled water after every bite now."

"Now Claudius nothing sweet, remember."

Kitty was not surprised that he scowled and said little, but she supposed Lady Constance meant well.

When the ladies returned to the drawing room, Miss Lucas and the three children went to their rooms. Kitty was quite touched when Pip and Sally hugged her goodnight. The food had been lovely and the house was warm. She sat by the fire and read by candle rather than tallow light, a luxury she really appreciated.

Dressed for bed, and just as she was combing her hair through, she remembered the lights she had lit in the schoolroom. Somebody probably had extinguished them. But what if they had not? What if a breeze sent a spark towards the paper? Reluctantly she tied a ribbon loosely around her hair and tightened the belt on her robe and returned to the schoolroom.

The lamps in the corridor had been extinguished, so it made sense that the schoolroom would be the same. Yet she could make out light spilling from underneath the door. Candle in one hand, and poker secured in her waistband she walked as quietly as she could though the poker hit her knee with every step. She wondered about the time of night. A she placed her hand on the door knob the poker banged against it.

The door was pulled open from the inside and she stumbled into two gentleman's hands. They grasped her firmly by the upper arm, steering the lit candle away from his clothing. She looked up into his face. Mr Gregory. Again.

"Miss Lucas, what the blazes ..." he hissed.

"Mr Gregory," she said in kind. "Why are we whispering?"

He pulled her inside and closed the door softly. He was still holding her one arm but as he moved she could see a desk laid out with empty jewellery settings and a set of small-handled tools.

As she strained to see, he loosened his grip and she walked forward. The settings were old and she instantly recognised them as the set worn by Lady Constance at dinner.

"If it is not too obvious a question, what is going on here?"

"I cannot deny it is a very pertinent question."

"In that case perhaps you would consider answering it?"

"Lady Constance invited me to dinner, when I came to enquire after her grandchildren. Do not worry I sang your praises."

"I am not worried. Why are you still here?"

"The gentlemen became engaged in a heated discussion of politics fuelled by some excellent brandy and since the hour was so late, Mr Fitzgerald invited me to stay the night."

"I wager the servants loved that."

"Why?"

"Never mind. Am I to assume then that you engineered to stay the night, so you could rob Lady Constance?"

"Hmm. Now I know why they say you should never explain yourself."

Feeling a draught Kitty turned around to see the curtain billowing. Closer inspection revealed an open window, and the light from a candle revealed a creeper allowing for easy entry or egress.

Closing the window, Kitty arranged herself next to the desk, putting the poker on the windowsill.

"I think an explanation is very much in order."

He ignored her demand and instead gave an admiring look. "You did not scream. That is quite remarkable in females of my acquaintance. Well done!"

She put her hand on the poker and looked squarely at him. His eyes were more grey now than blue. He was still immaculately dressed and had not changed since dinner. Though she did notice that in between rescuing her from brambles and turning up for dinner, he had managed a change, taking him from fashion plate to respectable and country. His expression had also changed and he now looked quite serious.

"Miss Lucas, where are the children?"

"In their ..."

In an instance she was at the door and with Mr Gregory

holding the candle behind her she opened the three doors in rapid succession. Each bed exhibited a lump. She turned to speak but stopped. Returning to the first room she entered quietly. It was gloomier in here as the fireplace was dark. Moving to the bed, she touched the sleeping body and waited. She then removed the cover in one flourish. Pillows and a bolster. She looked at the fireplace again as Mr Gregory lit the bedside candle. The painted fender glistened and she touched one finger to it. The fire had been doused with water from the jug. Mr Gregory held up a copy of the Iliad.

"Not Pip's."

"Not Pip's," she agreed.

She sat on the bed and picked up the book and started flicking through it absent-mindedly.

"The two incidents do not have to be connected," she said. "Claudius is clearly mollycoddled and may just have wanted a lark. A full moon, tonight. A poacher's moon."

"If that is the case," replied Mr Gregory, "he will return the way he left."

"Oh. I shut the window."

They set up vigil in the schoolroom. The fire was kindled, the lights doused and the window re-opened.

"Why am I not rousing Lady Constance, or you awakening Mr Fitzgerald?"

"Hmm?" Mr Gregory sat with his feet on the tiles and his eyes closed. Kitty sat bolt upright; the impropriety suddenly coming home to her. Not only was she alone with a man she was not related to, but her attire was somewhat informal. As she opened her mouth to speak there was a scraping noise outside the window.

Mr Gregory was now all attention. He put out an arm to stay her rising from her chair as the curtain billowed and a muddy boot appeared, closely followed by its twin. Mr Gregory's hand retreated from her arm and he started to relax. The feet placed themselves on the floor as a figure bent in two and started to unlace them. Her eyes were fixed on the boots. Well maintained, good quality but a little scraped with a slight covering of brick dust and moss. She was surprised that she could make out such detail in the firelight, when she realised that Mr Gregory had lit the light.

"Good evening," he began, placing himself between the bent over figure and the window.

Claudius stood and glanced at the window and then towards the door as Kitty placed herself in front of that. The blush started at his neck and then stained the rest of his face. They seemed to stand for an age looking at the boy before he sat at the desk in front of the remains of Lady Constance's necklaces.

"Where did you get the tools, Claudius?" asked Mr Gregory in a surprisingly gentle voice.

"Mr Bostock."

"And where are the jewels now?"

"Mr Bostock."

And with that Mr Gregory left the room, leaving both Claudius and Kitty staring after him. They followed his footsteps downstairs, across the hall and listened as the key in the front door turned and then opened and shut. No other sound troubled the household. Kitty turned her attention to Claudius.

"How much did he give you?" she asked.

"Nothing. It's not like that."

"Then what is it like?"

"I don't want to go to Oxford. I want to go home."

"This is not your home?"

"No. Father is in Jamaica."

"I thought Mr Bostock was preparing you for Oxford?"

"He is. He was going to help by buying my passage. Then

instead of going to Oxford I could go South and I'd get a boat home."

Claudius was the most animated she'd seen him and she could tell he was quite taken with the plan.

"But now it's all ruined!" And with a return to form he flounced out of the room leaving Kitty to look at the pieces of metal and wonder what next. Should she hide them, take them and the tale to Lady Constance or wait for Mr Gregory? Her first impulse was to protect Claudius but common sense told her that the loss would be discovered and that she was the stranger here. She raked the coals snubbed the light and returned to her bed.

She awoke to pandemonium. The window to the library had been jimmied and books and ornaments strewn around. The same was true of the drawing room and dining room where items of silver were missing. All this news was carried in the air by excited maids and adorned by the shrills of Lady Constance's maid as jewellery was found missing. Pip and Sally were enjoying the excitement but Claudius looked confused. Passing all three, Kitty made for the schoolroom. All was shipshape apart from an extra poker leaning on a firedog.

By the end of the morning Mr Fitzgerald reported the final tally: three necklaces, two snuffboxes and a cruet set. Loitering by Mr Fitzgerald's bookcases, Kitty saw Mr Gregory leaving on horseback, but was not in time to intercept him. By luncheon, the butler reported that the head gardener had found necklaces devoid of their jewels. By late afternoon, a most disturbing piece of news arrived. Mr Bostock, the curate, had been found unconscious from a knock to the head in the dining room of the vicarage. It was universally decided that he had disturbed the very same thieves in his own house, who had burgled The Towers, as a bag containing the jewels and silver lay by his side.

By the end of the day, Kitty felt that she was going to burst with frustration. Claudius and Mr Gregory, who had returned after luncheon, having both successfully avoided her the entire day, though she had caught sight of them both walking in the garden heads together.

Dinner that evening was taken in the schoolroom by Kitty, Sally and Pip.

"Is Claudius not joining us?"

"No. I heard Grandfather telling Grandmother that Uncle Philip wants Claudius back home. So no to Oxford and yes to the open seas," said Pip.

"Has he left already?"

"No, but he's left the schoolroom." And with that both children turned their attention to the ministrations of the cook.

Kitty looked wistfully at The Towers as she bobbed along in the small carriage. The country-made contraption had little in common with the maroon sprung beast which sat outside the entrance. While the black Welsh cob's jaunty gait had even less in common with the four beautifully matched chestnut ladies being walked up and down by their grooms. Claudius would be leaving in style.

Feeling the absence of her grandson even before he had left, Lady Constance had decided she would take the children back to school personally. So, after an eventful three days, Kitty was on the road again. The Towers was her ideal house. Not too old or big to be rambling, it was fashionable and comfortable. No badly swept chimneys or need for economy meant that fires were lit where they were required. Smashed vases caused by exuberant ball games were swept away with a sigh and a pat on the head. A very comfortable life, and one from which she was excluded.

Her destination was the coach, which left the Church Inn a

little after noon. John, the driver, had the family's letters to deliver, and now Kitty too. Perched alongside, neither was talkative, one keeping the cob in hand, and the other re-jigging her plans now she had a week to herself. The sensible approach would be to travel home, spend Easter with father, then back to London to Aunt Charlotte. But she had already said her farewells at home and going back would seem something of an anti-climax, not to say an expense. Lady Constance had paid her the agreed sum with a little extra for the inconvenience and, for the first time in her life, Kitty had some money and time to call her own.

The bustle of the inn came too soon for any plan to be formed, the ticket was bought and paid for by John, and she was soon handed up into the carriage while bundles, trunks, boxes, sacks and passengers were wedged firmly on top. A whip cracked, the carriage surged forward and they were off.

Two country men made uncomfortable by their starched clothes sat opposite and a woman sitting next to Kitty had had the foresight to bring a heated brick for her feet and a blanket for her legs. There wasn't very much room inside the carriage so Kitty got her share of both, for which she was grateful. She also received a complete history of Mrs Wiley's family – a husband, five children and six grandchildren, and Mr Wiley's fortunes as a farmer and merchant in seeds and agrarian equipment. Thankfully, Mrs Wiley needed little in the way of encouragement to talk, apart from an open countenance and a smile, which Kitty accomplished while her mind wandered.

She found herself in somewhat of a quandary as in all good books - in all the books she had read - she knew she should be feeling excited and ready for an adventure, which would arrive in the form of a mysterious stranger, a lost letter, a hidden gem. or tragic accident. What she actually felt was an almost overwhelming sense of being alone.

Mrs Wiley had run out of steam and her head was now

drooping onto her chest. The men opposite now have their hats over their faces and their chests rose gently and in unison. The other four occupants she supposed to be farmers and were involved in an interesting game consisting of a board of wood with holes drilled in it, a set of short sticks and a pack of cards. They obviously knew each other well as their conversation was a series of grunts and nods which told them (and no one else) exactly what was needed. Singing and larking about came from the roof, but Kitty had forgotten to look who was lodged up there with her bags.

John had made sure that she got a corner seat, but apart from that had not paid her any heed. But she was grateful as she could gaze out at the fields and beginnings of spring. Snowdrops were dotted around the banks but there was little sign of life in the trees which seemed as dormant as in February, while the fields looked sodden and morose. To complement her mood the clouds won their battle against the sun. It had been a hard winter and wasn't giving up its hold until it had to.

Fences, outbuildings, houses and then streets came into view as they arrived in town. The stop at the inn here was brief – just enough to change the horses. In that ten minutes the passengers had to make their own arrangements for food and comfort. True, the inn and other entrepreneurs were ready for them with pies, flasks and hot bricks, but the prices reflected the quick turnaround, and Kitty could see why frequent travellers brought their own provisions.

Being raised to trust no pie she hadn't seen the makings of, she bought half a dozen apples, wrinkled but firm, a hunk of farmhouse cheese, and a couple of warm nutty bread cakes. The price was shocking. She spied a dairy maid and haggled a quart of milk for one of the bread cakes, before treating herself to a mug of mulled cider. Thus fortified, Kitty prepared to re-board the carriage, when whispered voices caught her attention.

The place was full of sound; ostlers calling to one another, drivers screaming abuse, sellers advertising their wares and travellers trying to find one another – so why bother to whisper? Intrigued, she stopped on the steps, jumped down and prepared to follow an imaginary lost apple in the direction of the whisperers. She couldn't make out words but the speech was clipped and well educated with a touch of arrogance discernible through the whispers and a hint of a stammer which became more pronounced as the discussion grew heated. Crouching behind the wheels of a carriage, her adventure was stopped abruptly by the sound of the horn from the Mail.

Coming to her senses, Kitty scuttled back the way she had come, but as she did so she spotted two pairs of boots belonging to the conspirators – one with creamy tassels the like of which she had only ever seen on curtains, and one so shiny you could see reflections from the wheels in them.

"Cooeee. Over here dear, I've saved you your seat near the window. I know that you young ones like the scenery. Well, so do we old 'uns, and Mr Kettle was all for sitting there. But I told him you'd be here any minute and he was not to move one bit. Not right at all for a young girl like you sitting next to a young man all unmarried like. There we are, all snug as a bug in a rug. Oh, off we go then. Now did I tell you …"

Kitty hadn't realised she had fallen asleep until she was jolted awake and her head banged into the window frame. There was consternation from inside the carriage and screams from the top as the coach juddered to a standstill. One glance out of the window showed her that this was not a scheduled stop. Shouts and curses followed, then the door was opened and one of the farmers, Mr Kettle, jumped out. As Kitty made a move to stand, Mrs Wiley laid a hand on her knee, "No dear, best not." Looking up, Kitty saw that the farmer's wife had lost her smile. Before she could enquire more, a body was forced in through the door by Mr Kettle and she presumed some of the men riding on top. Mr Kettle then shut the door and she saw his legs as they climbed onto the roof.

The body was of a young man. Kitty sat there in silence as her fellow passengers wordlessly forced brandy between his lips and Mrs Wiley put her brick under his feet and blanket over his bloodied waistcoat. Bloodied! She opened her mouth only to have Mrs Wiley take a horn beaker from one of the farmers and bid her to drink. Her passengers looked serious, but not as taken aback as she was.

"Not uncommon around here, miss. The road's well-known for it. Just surprised the coachman stopped – he'll be docked wages if anyone complains," explained one of the other farmers.

"Why would anyone complain?" she began as the coach lurched forward and bowled along faster than ever. She hung onto the seat and wedged herself tightly in the corner.

The new passenger groaned slightly and after a while she forced herself to look at him. He was quite young, his clothes looked expensive, and his face was very white. Heroines, she knew, would know exactly what to do, how to organise the stunned and panicking passengers, and nurse the rich and grateful young man back to health before the coach reached its destination. Reality was different. Her passengers knew exactly what to do, while she sat in the corner. She had seen injuries before and had nursed a few. What stunned her was the matter-of-fact way everyone was dealing with the incident. No indignation, or even surprise, as if this was an everyday occurrence. Then it hit her, it *was* an everyday occurrence. She was the one out of place here. Her upbringing hadn't prepared her for anything like this.

It was dark when the coach pulled into the Red Lion in the

market town of Epsom. The injured boy was taken out of the carriage and her companions left, too. Mrs Wiley gave orders for the safe disposition of her boxes, before turning to Kitty and enveloping her in a hug. "You take care, my girl."

She stood in the courtyard. The coach was changing horses and passengers for the return journey. But what about her? She could carry on to London on the Mail which left at midnight – very auspicious – and then what? At present she was in the way, so she moved towards the inn as there seemed nowhere else to go.

Within twenty minutes she was ensconced in a tidy, clean bedroom with a good fire and the promise of a meal in half an hour and a bed for two nights. As she was making arrangements, she had seen well-turned out men and women availing themselves of private parlours and seen the general dining room – the landlady hadn't given her either of these options nor told her that a hot meal would be served in her room. Kitty supposed such a lady was used to weighing up the needs of her customers and wondered if she should ask her what to do with the rest of her life too!

A knock on her door brought her to her feet and saved her from indulging in a good bout of self-pity. The man standing there carried a leather bag and had slightly bloodied cuffs on his shirt sleeves, rather than being some reprobate, she recognised that he must be the doctor.

"Ah, good evening, miss, I was led to believe you were in the coach which brought in the injured boy?"

She blushed, how could she have forgotten him? "I was, sir."

The doctor continued, now fiddling with his bag: "I've given him a draught and he'll need another in the morning." He thrust a brown bottle at her.

"But I don't even know him!"

"No one does, but the place is too busy to trust anyone else with his medication. Tell Mrs Pound that I'll pop back after the last race."

And with that he put his hat on his head and left, almost bumping into a morose girl dressed in grey bearing a tray of steaming food.

The girl appeared to be about fourteen and introduced herself as Poppy – which Kitty did not think the most appropriate of names. She had plopped herself on the bed while Kitty ate and showed no intention of moving.

The food was good and there was a great deal of it – slices of roast chicken and mutton with carrots and suede and fluffy potatoes topped with brown glistening gravy. The apple pie and cream went down well too, but Kitty did feel she wouldn't be able to eat for a week. All the time Poppy sat swinging her legs and playing with the frayed threads of her apron.

"Poppy, where is the young man who came in from my coach?"

"Next door, miss. Mrs Pound and me had to wash him down for the doctor. Do you want to see him?"

That wasn't the top of her list of entertainments for the evening, but then there was nothing on her list.

"Don't you have to get back to work? I don't want to get you into trouble?"

"Ah, no one will miss me."

Crashing plates and shouts from below made that seem uncertain, but Kitty brushed the crumbs from her skirt and smiled. "Yes, I will see him."

If anything, the boy looked even younger then she had thought. His breathing was rapid and shallow. Kitty knew this was not a good sign. His forehead was clammy and the paleness of his skin was heightened by two red patches on his cheeks.

"Poppy, can you fetch the little red box from my room? Oh, and some hot water?"

By the time Poppy had returned, Kitty had the tiny window open, more than one meagre candle lit, and was wiping down his face and neck. Opening the box, Kitty took out a vial and dripped a few drops of oil into the hot water. A pungent smell filtered into the room. Poppy looked on open-mouthed.

"Tincture of Benzoin. It helps breathing, though I usually only use it if I have a cold. You better be getting back. I'll stay until he's looking better."

Poppy's new-found respect coaxed a bobbed curtsey from her as she left – leaving the door ajar for the sake of propriety.

Although his breathing deepened and his cheeks took on a more natural colour, Kitty was loathe to leave him for long. She popped back for a shawl, a pillow and her book. Settling herself into the chair next to the bed she read and dozed through the night. She was aware of the call for the Mail, and the ensuing hustle and bustle but it didn't disturb her or her patient.

As the quality of light outside changed, so too did the amount of movement in the kitchen and courtyard. Her patient was sleeping in a more natural position. Kitty rearranged his covers then removed herself and her belongings, closing the door gently behind her.

The linen on her bed was old but clean and smelt of lavender. It reminded Kitty of home. A gentle scratching on her door roused her a little and then the door opened. Had she forgotten to lock it?

"Good morning, miss, the missus sent me up with some breakfast. Shall I put it here?"

Kitty looked at the girl, who smiled.

"Your hair's funny."

Kitty looked at her sharply but bit back a tart reply, the girl didn't really need. The bitten nails, scuff mark around her neck and shielded eyes told Kitty that Poppy did not have a pleasant life. And as she put the tray on the table by the fire, her rolled-up sleeves revealed bruises the size and shape of fingers. No, Poppy was not cared for.

"What shall we do about the boy, miss?"

Poppy sat on the arm of the chair while Kitty pulled on her robe, shoes and tried to tame her 'funny' hair with her hands and a ribbon.

"Is he awake?"

"How should I know?"

Kitty turned and walked to her patient's room. The bed covers were half on the floor and the boy splayed on the bed. He wore a clean, but old, bed-shirt. His hair was plastered to his head, yet as she touched his forehead with the back of her hand it was cool and dry; at her touch his eyes flew open.

He didn't quite scream, but Poppy did as Kitty jumped back. As the boy scrambled to get his covers, he stopped, groaned and fell back.

"You were found by the road," Kitty informed him. "Are you hungry?"

She took the croak as a yes and sent Poppy for sustenance. Kitty then took some time sorting out his covers and helping him sit propped up by pillows while keeping up a flow of talk about the sheets, fire, size of window and clear blue skies she could just see out of the small window. No curtains she noticed. On Poppy's return she told her to help him eat while she returned to her room to dress and eat her own breakfast.

He really wasn't her responsibility she told herself as she looked at the tincture sitting on the mantelpiece. Was the doctor a gambling man or employed by a trainer? She knew Epsom for its horses and some of the cant from her cousin Joseph. Or was he a human doctor at all? Most owners would employ a vet for their horses if push came to shove but a

doctor for the jockeys? She decided against using the draught –
after all the boy seemed well, if stiff and in pain. But what of
his parents? Where were they?

"No one knows, miss. The magistrate has been informed."
Mrs Pound informed her when questioned by Kitty.

She also wheedled out of her that the magistrate had agreed
to pay for his stay as his clothes showed him to be 'well-heeled'.
A few more compliments about the quality of the cured ham
she had eaten for breakfast earned her the information that a
letter to Bow Street had been dispatched to London on the
night mail.

Intrigued, and having no plans, Kitty informed Mrs Pound
that she would be staying until the end of the week before
meeting her aunt in London. Mr Pound arrived then to give
her a list of interesting places in the vicinity that most casual
visitors would miss in their rush to get to the capital.

Bickering and laughter greeted her as she returned upstairs.
Entering the invalid's room, she saw Poppy and her patient
playing with a kitten.

"Where did that come from?"

"Jem, the stable cat. They'll be drowned as soon as anyone
realises. But John says he'll have Snowball."

"Tiger," said a croaky voice.

Deciding to ignore the cat, Kitty continued: "John. is it?
Well, John, do you remember what happened to you?"

"Not really."

"Where are your parents?"

"Italy?"

"Someone is going to be concerned about you? Who should
we tell?"

John shrugged his shoulders, "Dr Parkin, I suppose."

While quite capable and willing to transport and manage
the Bentley children, this she was not being paid for. Kitty

walked back to her own room, collected her writing case and deposited it on John's bed.

"Write to him," she commanded and went for a soothing walk to the old church.

Just as the landlord had informed her, it was a fine example of medieval architecture. As she walked along the High Street, she was reminded that this was a spa town full of the fashionable in search of health and entertainment. There were a variety of establishments devoted to the health-giving waters, shops to cater for the well-to-do, and some very impressive houses and lodgings. At least Aunt Charlotte wouldn't be able to complain that the venue was unsuitable. An informative visit to a little shop set up as a museum, and a pretty bottle of Epsom Salts for her aged relative saw Kitty Lucas restored and resolved on her course of action.

On returning from her walk, she arranged for John's letter to be sent. She had then arranged for new clothes for him and use of the parlour. Her funds didn't stretch to such generosity, but Mr and Mrs Pound agreed that the magistrate would be happy to fund it since the address was only in Bath. The Red Lion also boasted a small orchard to the side of the stables; a remnant of when it had been a farm, Kitty guessed. Although the weather was far from warm, it gave somewhere for them to walk and she was a firm believer in the healing powers of fresh air.

Kitty took the role of older sister ensuring that John slept and ate. His increased complaining reassured her that he was recovering as did the different hues his bruises were exhibiting. Poppy was more with them than not. Kitty didn't want to discourage her but knew that Poppy may well have to pay for her truancy. Mrs Pound did seem a decent woman but someone had made bruises on Poppy's arm.

Things came to a head on the fourth day. Kitty was in her room writing a letter to her father, when she heard shouts coming from downstairs, not unusual in a busy inn. But the screams were different and she hurried out of the room and down the back stairs to the pantry. A lad in moleskin trousers, leather gaiters and a stained jerkin was holding Poppy by her hair and hitting her with a belt.

Mrs Pound and Kitty entered the room from opposite doors at the same time and as they both started to shout – someone leapt on Poppy's assailant and pummelled him to the floor. It was John, but he had the wrong size, weight and experience to indulge in an all-out brawl. Poppy was no swooning maid and gathering a wooden butter pat in each hand started boxing the ears of the stable lad now astride John. Mrs Pound grabbed Poppy around the waist and Kitty threw a bucket of water over the two boys.

William, it appeared, was Poppy's brother and worked as an ostler. He had come for Poppy's wages to take home to find that she had bought a new apron and ribbon for her hair. Poppy was sent to sort herself out with instructions to then clean the pantry, thoroughly. William was given to the tender mercies of Mr Henry who ran the livery and John was left with Kitty.

"Just what were you thinking?"

"He had no right to talk to Poppy like that and …"

"And John…?"

He leant on her as they went back upstairs and she led him in silence to his room. Mrs Pound having restored order downstairs, followed with clothes, hot water, a glass of brandy and liniment. Between them they changed his shirt and cleaned him up. She left Kitty to apply the liniment – a piece of straw attached to the bottom giving a clue as to its previous patient. Were all human and horse ailments treated the same here? Kitty was worried, John seemed exhausted from his chivalric encounter. He sipped some brandy, which brought a little colour back to pale cheeks but he had problems focusing and offered no resistance when he was settled back into his bed.

Opening the window and lighting a candle, she drank the soup a subdued Poppy had brought them. The girl could not meet her eyes, though she still wore the offending ribbon in her hair. Kitty had moved herself back to John's room just like the first night at the inn. Something in the back of her head said she shouldn't let him sleep, so she had decided to rouse him every hour. He didn't want the soup, but Kitty managed to get a few more drops of brandy down him.

She heard coaches arrive and the night Mail clamouring for attention. She listened to the coachmen and stable lads' shouts and happy customers wending their way home as she walked about the room to keep herself awake. She was rousing him for the umpteenth time when he responded, "For goodness sake, let me sleep." Tugging the covers from her, he turned on his side.

Smiling, she left.

# A NEW DIRECTION

And so she was on the road again. This time with a young girl and boy but with the added pleasure of a kitten which alternated periods of mad chasing with intense sleeping.

After a flurry of letters between her and Dr Parkin, at a quite select education facility for boys in Bath, she had been engaged to act as the responsible adult for delivering John St John to the hands of his rightful guardians. His home was in Oulton in the West Riding of Yorkshire and his parents were indeed in Italy. With his antecedents cleared up, and a letter to her aunt to explain the delay in her arrival, everything should have been plain sailing.

However, the sick boy was starting to show his true colours as his convalescence gave way to boredom and mischief.

"Miss Lucas, I know you're not his guardian like and that the poor mite coulda died – twice. But if I find him in the malt one more time, I won't be responsible for my actions. What he needs is a good hiding!"

"But Miss Lucas, my nurse always said that malt extract was good for you when you were sick."

"I do not think that she meant for you to eat it by the spoonful."

"Oh, I didn't have a spoon – I just used my fingers."

The removal to Bath could not come soon enough. She was quite excited about a detour to Bath, a city her friends had described as a place devoted to pleasant conversation, picnics and shopping, with the odd nod towards a health cure. In her mind's eye the pavements glittered with acolytes of Beau Brummell, articulate, intelligent and only concerned with the finer things in life. She studiously ignored the voice in her head which reminded her that life was never that tidy.

As they were about to leave, Poppy appeared with battered bandbox, patched cloak and wriggling kitten. She was adamant that they had to take the kitten or it would be drowned, and that she had to go with Kitty as she needed a maid to be respectable. Poppy found allies in Mrs Pound and John, and thus thoroughly outmanoeuvred, Kitty was on her way.

The journey was more pleasant than the stage had been and since Poppy and John amused each other, her only task was to keep the peace over disagreements about whose turn it was, or whether the Heart was trump. Horses were changed every ten miles or so and John and Poppy took it in turns to use the pull-down seat. However, by the time they slowed their pace to enter a particularly busy set of streets John was pale and quiet, his previous exertions still affecting his stamina.

"Are we there yet?" asked Poppy.

"This is Hungerford. We'll stay at the inn tonight and set off again first thing."

Poppy was glued to the window. Kitty found herself daunted by the number of gigs, long wagons and chaises jostling their way through the streets. If this was Hungerford, what would Bath be like? And what about London? At last they turned off the road and into a yard where the calls between postillions, drivers and ostlers became louder and, to Kitty's ears, more graphic.

The Great West Road was so smooth on the final leg to Bath that both her charges nodded off. Poppy's head rested gently on John's shoulder but it seemed that at any minute it was going to fall onto his lap or the floor. She was about to intervene when John woke slightly changing his position to make both of them comfortable and secure. Kitty smiled at the bucolic image but with misgivings. John's well-cut hair falling over his eyes was shining in the afternoon sun while Poppy's was matted in parts and secured under a second-hand bonnet. The fact that John didn't seem to care said a lot about his upbringing but also about how innocent he was about society's expectations and judgements.

When the gait of the horses changed she knew they were entering Bath. Mrs Pound had recommended the Westgate and so it was in the late afternoon that they arrived feeling grimy, tetchy and very hungry.Dr Parkin was short, be-wigged, be-spectacled and putting some strain on the middle buttons of his waistcoat. His clothing would have been appropriate a decade previously but was clean and well ordered. He greeted them in a private parlour that he had booked for their arrival, and she noticed from the table beside him he had been indulging in tea and a copy of John Simpson's *A Complete System of Cookery* rather than the other allurements of the inn. He was so reminiscent of her father, Kitty felt a lump in her throat.

"Miss Lucas? I must admit to expecting someone a little older." And straight to the point – again just like her father. "St John, good to see you. Are you ready?"

"Sir, I would like to show Poppy the school."

"Certainly. Miss Lucas and I have a few items to discuss."

With a short time given to transferring baggage, freshening of faces and toilet, and a fresh pot of tea, the whole party were in the doctor's carriage and heading through the byways of Bath towards Bathwick Hill and the modern villa which was the home of Dr Parkin's academy. He had visibly warmed to Kitty as they discussed the classics during the journey. Most of his students were being prepared for an Oxford education, but though he talked in detail about Homer, Kitty could tell he was distracted.

Honey-coloured stone and fresh paint were her first impressions of the building and she could tell by the smile on John's face when he saw an older lady in a lace cap that the boy would be looked after. Mrs Titherington tutted and organised and scooted Poppy and John (and kitten) into the rear of the house. Kitty could hear voices and laughter greet their arrival, as she was shown into a room lined with books, deep chairs and a smouldering log in the fireplace.

"Is there a problem, Dr Parkin?"

"We think there might be, Miss Lucas," said a voice from within one of the deep chairs facing the fire. The voice sounded very familiar as she turned to face it, a servant entered with refreshments forestalling the rather forthright comment that threatened to escape her lips.

"Miss Lucas, may I introduce Mr Gregory."

Kitty didn't trust herself to respond so responded with a small bow. As she lifted her head she saw the door closing behind as both the servant and Dr Parkin left the room.

Without asking, Mr Gregory poured a glass of Orgeat and handed her a slice of seed cake. Very good seed cake. The sweet almond orange beverage was quite refreshing too. However, she eyed his glass of Madeira with longing.

"I must congratulate you on keeping your council over the Claudius affair. It all turned out quite satisfactorily."

"Are young boys in trouble a speciality?"

"So blunt and we are co-conspirators."

"What have you said to Dr Parkin? This meeting is quite inappropriate."

"Never fear, your reputation is quite safe. It is your gender and demeanour I require, not your virtue."

She knew he meant this to sound reassuring but instead found herself quite put out. She realised he was speaking to her again.

"May I enquire as to your immediate plans?"

"I will be leaving for London. My Aunt Charlotte has been expecting me for some days now."

"Do you want to go?"

"I beg your pardon. I do not think—"

"I want you to care for the boy while I solve a puzzle for which you might have useful insights. I'm sure you can give me a couple of days before you have to meet your Aunt Charlotte in London."

There was no question in this and what she had meant to say was that her aunt would be expecting her and that she had business to attend to before she began the next leg of her journey. But she was intrigued and flattered as he knew she would be. She recognised only too well that she was being manipulated.

He took her silence for agreement.

"Then we have no time to waste. Did St John mention Patrick at all?"

"No. not a word. Why?"

"Two boys went missing. Both are well connected so kidnapping cannot be dismissed. There had been no news about either until your communication to Dr Parkin."

The door opened and Mrs Titherington entered with a maid to clear the things.

"Mary's putting a supper out in the small dining room for you, Miss Lucas. Oh, Mr Gregory, Mr Clark was asking for you."

## A PUZZLE UNFOLDS

Kitty spent a restless night. Images of carriages, balloons and children just out of her reach kept her on the edge of sleep and waking. However, the morning started bright with toasted bread and hot chocolate in bed.

With no sign of Poppy, Kitty dressed herself. Just as she was about to leave her bedchamber, Mrs Titherington appeared and took Kitty to an area set out as a classroom, where St John was showing Poppy a globe: "They used to think California was an island, but see they found out what it really looked like and glued it on. One day I'll visit Africa and find out what is there. I'll send you the piece to glue on."

Kitty noted microscopes and a copy of the Iliad. Dr Parkin was a rationalist and classicist and a glance at Poppy's face showed Kitty that she knew her fledging friendship with John was over. They lived in different worlds and, in hers, globes were something to be dusted not dreamed about.

"Poppy, we need to ask John some questions." Mr Gregory had appeared silently behind them.

Kindly, Mrs Titherington took her out with the promise of

honey. Dr Parkin tidied away the globe and busied himself with organising the contents of a desk.

"John, tell me about Patrick."

John brushed a lock of hair from his eyes. The colourful effects of the beating were wearing off and the smile he wore found its way to a twinkle and a dimple. The scamp was about to be re-born.

"He's my friend. Has been since we came here the same day. Rodgers said we were like twins because we always did the same things, finished each other's sentences and—" He broke off.

"And?" Kitty asked gently.

"Well we did each other's work at times. Dr Parkin finds it hard to tell us apart."

"How about other people?"

"Well, we did like to dress the same."

"What about the day you left here?" enquired Mr Gregory.

"We were going to go to Sir William Hershel 's lecture on astronomy, but Patrick hadn't finished his Latin translation. He really wanted to go, so. Well we swapped. When I finished his Latin, I went for a walk in the garden."

"Then?" she prompted.

"I don't know. It went dark. Then I remember falling and it hurt."

John was starting to look distressed and glancing from one adult to the next. Dr Parkin, put down the inkwell he was polishing and started to move forward. Mr Gregory put a hand out to detain him.

"John," he started.

"Where is Patrick?" interrupted John.

"John," repeated Mr Gregory, "Patrick, disappeared the day

after you did. When we heard you had been found, we hoped he would be too. But there is no sign. We need your help."

The four of them walked towards the garden to retrace the boy's steps. Under Mr Gregory's guidance, Kitty and Dr Parkin walked a few steps behind where they could see Mr Gregory's guiding hand on the small of John's back. He signalled them to halt their progress when they came to a sapling. The grass was close-cropped and saplings had been planted in a seemingly random manner.

They were at the top of a small rise, the house behind them and the road below shielded by a wall which in its turn was softened by evergreen shrubs.

"Are those rhododendron, Dr Parkin?"

"Yes, unusual are they not? Are you a botanist Miss Lucas?"

"No sir, although my father followed the endeavours of Sir Joseph Banks with interest."

"As you may notice we follow a more modern curriculum here for the boys. That seems to attract a special kind of parent of a more adventurous bent. Look."

With that he led her towards a small sapling with delicate leaves.

"Palmatum from Japan. One of our parents brought us two samples for cultivation inside but I thought I would try one here. Quite successful though very slow growing."

"Do all the boys' parents ..." Her question trailed off as she noticed Mr Gregory and John running down the slope towards to bushes.

Decorum and age meant that she and Dr Parkin travelled at a more sedate pace. So much so that when they caught up they saw the two dragging a piece of sacking out of the greenery. Well used, it lay on the floor while the four of them stared at it accusingly.

"Is it relevant, sir?"

Mr Gregory held it to his nose feeling the threads as he did so.

"Hard to tell at this moment. But let us err on the side of caution and take it with us."

And with that he strode back up the slope and towards the house, his audience following at their own pace. Kitty tried not to be worried about her now muddied shoes. To his relief, John was released to Mrs Titherington while Kitty and Dr Parkin were subject to quite an unusual proposition.

"Mesmerism?"

"I admit it does sound quite shocking, but really it is just an intense piece of concentration screening out distractions to allow the memory to fully assert itself. Any information St John can give us at this point has to be more than we know now."

"I would have to be present," countered Dr Parkin.

Kitty said nothing initially. This was something completely out of her experience and she wanted nothing to do with it. However, she suspected that neither of the two men in the room with her had John's well-being as their principle concern. The ends justified the means for them both; Edward Gregory had a child to find though she didn't know quite why, and Dr Parkin was understandably concerned for the future of his school as well as the boy; scandal was something to be avoided at all costs.

They continued their plans and she listened. Her engagement was over, she could just walk away at this point and continue with her life. She rationalised that she would stay for John so that when the good doctor went to fetch him, she nonchalantly picked up a discarded book on journeys through Italy. Then addressed Mr Gregory directly.

"What do you want to achieve with this, Mr Gregory? You haven't explained who Patrick is to you."

"I have been asked by his family to look for him. Initially I was looking for two children, now it is just the one and St John is the only lead I have, Miss Lucas. I have explained all this to Dr Parkin."

Kitty was not about to take the hint and leave the matter alone, "And what effect will this have on the boy?"

"It will allow him to help in his friend's recovery."

Turning his back on her, Mr Gregory showed he had finished with the conversation, much in the style of the old king. After all it was a waste of time to explain anything to a mere woman. She bit her lip and kept her peace.

Dr Parkin returned with John who was looking pale but smiled when he saw her sitting there. She returned the smile and put her book on a side table. Mr Gregory pulled two chairs to face each other and sat in one indicating that John should sit in the other. Accepting the nod from Dr Parkin, John took his place. Holding the hessian sack between them Mr Gregory pushed the sacking into his face.

"Breathe deeply and concentrate."

Mr Gregory's voice was cold and insistent, and within a very few minutes John was struggling against the sacking. His breathing was fast and shallow and he seemed in distress. Dr Parkin made to stand, but Kitty followed the action though kneeling in front of the boy, annoyed and surprised at how Mr Gregory could not see that this would be hard for the child.

"It is quite all right John. You are safe, I am here. I will take the sacking away. Tell me what you can see and hear. We need to know so we can find your friend. You are safe and we will find him, too."

Smiling weakly, John spoke "I can hear shouting and horses shuffling. Oh, a post horn!" He looked straight at her. "I can smell mash and tallow smoke, too." He beamed. "Is that where he is?"

Gregory spoke now. "We don't know yet. Is there any light? What can you see?"

John described an enclosure which could be a store room or a stable. He did remember that there were reeds on the floor, not straw and this sent Mr Gregory heading towards the door.

"Excellent, Miss Lucas. I'll be back tomorrow."

And he was gone.


After a brief consultation with Mrs Titherington, Poppy was helping Kitty freshen herself up for dinner. The whole experience was taking on a dreamlike quality for her, especially as everyone else seemed to take to their allotted roles with ease. Poppy was the quiet and polite maid, John St John the schoolboy, Mr Gregory the man of the world and Dr Parkin the wise teacher. As she stepped into the room for dinner and caught the eye of Mrs Titheringon, she recognised that there was at least one person in the building who thought that they were teetering between melodrama and tragedy.

They were eating in a large dining room with all the boys at two long tables while the adults were seated on a separate table, raised on a dais. There were some lovely framed watercolours on the walls and closer inspection showed that they were by the boys – past and present she assumed from the names and years on little brass plaques on the frames. There was a fire in the hearth and candles rather than tallows on the tables. A quick head count gave her 18 boys while the top table was laid for eight. The food was wholesome, and both staff and children ate the same. It was a pleasant atmosphere, with the boys being subdued rather than cowed. As she toyed with her food she noticed that under the veneer of perfect manners, shells and stones were being swapped and practical jokes played. As she relinquished her plate, she spotted Dr Parkin who with a look was putting the stop to a more exuberant practical joke involving a tack. Kitty felt that this was an unusual establishment in more ways than one.

As no one saw to fill in the details Kitty was left to make use her friendship with John and Poppy to find out the facts of the situation. Patrick Templeton was the only son of Sophia and Thomas. An adventurous pair, they had both been lost during a storm on their return from a visit to Hanover five years earlier. Patrick was the ward of his uncle, Geraint Templeton-Hughes. And while he was rarely seen at the school, his son often visited but received mixed reviews relayed to her via the kitchen and stable by Poppy

"He's a one miss, very pretty but very handy with the servants when he visits."

"A real swell Miss Lucas. He has the best horses ever and never the same ones."

It was approaching noon three days later when Mr Gregory and his servant reappeared. All interested parties bar Poppy and John were in the library.

Though still immaculately turned out, Mr Gregory's boots were dusty, his necktie not the freshest, and a shadow was on the chin of the gentleman of fashion. This slipping of the mask of urbane gentleman endeared him more to Miss Lucas than the elaborate boots and sardonic fashionable manner.

"I do have news. A relation of Patrick's has been combing the country near the family home in case he was making his way home and, unfortunately, he was unhorsed in the process and has damaged his shoulder and knee, and is house-bound for several days. He believes the boy had run away from school and I have promised to keep him informed. I have also matched post-houses and stabling and come up with two possible hostelries in the vicinity for which I will require St John to accompany me. And you too, of course, Miss Lucas."

This announcement caused uproar. Immediately a heated debate developed between Dr Parkin, Mrs Titherington and Mr Gregory about the suitability of John going on such a journey.

"He is hardly recovered from his last encounter," said Mrs Titherington.

"His parents left him in our care and charge, but I do not believe this was their understanding of *loco parentis*," added Dr Parkin.

Though no one would have known from her calm exterior, there were warring emotions at work in Kitty's breast too. She wanted to find out what had happened and this without doubt was the most exciting thing that had ever happened to her, but indignation was winning. No one had asked; they had assumed, again, that she would put her plans on hold.

True, they were nothing compared to finding Patrick. But on the other hand, she was not a lady of independent means nor was she a servant, and certainly not his, to be commanded. If she was paid would that make her a servant? Excitement and wounded feelings vied for prominence.

Wearily, Mr Gregory stood. "My apologies. My tiredness has made me impatient. I understand your logic so now understand mine. Time is of the essence. If Patrick is not already dead he shortly will be. Forgive my bluntness. St John knows more than he thinks, but I don't have the temperament to coax it from him. That is your role Miss Lucas. I know St John's parents well and have their trust and they would insist on doing everything in their power to help. I will scrape the road from my clothes and we will leave after a quick meal if you would be so kind, Mrs Titherington."

He turned on his heel, bowed beautifully and left.

"George?" queried Mrs Titherington, looking at Dr Parkin.

"I believe he will keep St John safe and to be frank, Helen, could our school survive such a scandal should it become known?"

"I will pack and hurry up the kitchen."

Which left Kitty and Dr Parkin alone. She coughed. The kindly teacher looked at her and smiled. "Oh, I am sorry my dear, I forgot you were there." He peered closely at her. "And no one asked your opinion or requested your help, but this is not the time for wounded feelings. What arrangements do you need to make?"

As she left the library, a trunk was being carried to the hallway and a table laid in small drawing room next to the study. Dr Parkin was writing to her aunt as the truth would not do and she had not the time to think of a convincing scenario which would reassure her family. She needed to change and pack, so she quickened her step. Poppy was ahead of her, already alerted by Mrs Titherington, clothes were being rolled and folded hardly having had time to drop their creases. Poppy was dressed for travel, her bandbox positioned by the door.

In no time at all they were on the road yet again. Poppy and John dozed while Kitty held onto the leather strap as they trundled back to Bath. Mr Gregory rode alongside the carriage and she caught glimpses of his boot from time to time. Although the coach was hired, it was a good one; clean and well upholstered and the driver was none other than Pip's Runner, Clarky.

The first post-house they aimed for was the Black Bear. As usual no one saw fit to explain to her why but as she was told to get the children to the stables on some pretext, she decided it was time to start to employ her own insight. The now commonplace noises of such inns soon accosted her ears. The Bear was well-appointed, efficiently run and was entering one of the busiest times of day. Mr Gregory managed to acquire a private parlour and while Clarky saw to the horses, he summoned the landlord.

"Mr Cook, I believe?"

"At your service, sir."

"We are looking for a runaway and believe that he came this way about a week ago."

While Mr Gregory questioned the landlord, as arranged Kitty, John and Poppy made for the stables, adding for the benefit of the landlord: "John, how could you have been so silly. Poppy are you sure you saw it on the seat?"

The windowless corridor from the parlour led them downstairs and through the common room and out through the back to the stables. Clarky had apparently scouted out the layout on his first visit and so they walked with purpose, confidence and suppressed excitement. As Mr Gregory had schooled them on where to go, he added, "No one will ever question you if you move and speak as if you have the right to be there."

The cobbles were clear, but the gullies were filled with a variety of liquids and unspeakable lumps. Hoisting skirts to a higher, but respectable, height they strode forth. Away from the bustle of the main courtyard were three stalls, probably an overflow for busier days. Each was carpeted with reeds and by the entry were tallow holders built into the wall. Clarky was standing inside.

Nodding, he moved to the entrance and they moved into one of the stalls. Turning over a bucket she sat John down and crouched in front of him. She felt her heart fluttering but consciously kept her face and voice calm.

"Close your eyes and tell me if this feels familiar."

John's eyes were shut and he breathed slowly for several minutes before nodding.

"What can you see?"

"Horses."

"'Ardly surprisin' seein' as we're in a stable," muttered Poppy.

"Well they weren't any old horses so don't be so .... so ..." snapped John. And Poppy turned her shoulder to him and started making an informal pile of reeds with her toe.

"What was special about them?" asked a calm soft voice from behind them. She had not heard Mr Gregory enter but there he was. This trait of his was starting to irritate but she held her breath waiting for John's response.

"Their legs were really thick and soft and smelt funny and they had clothes on."

Poppy started to giggle.

Clarky turned on his heel and reached up over the door to a concealed shelf. He dropped down a bundle of old clothes. As it unrolled itself he picked up a hood with a long snout. Looking at Mr Gregory he added, "And the leg bindings for protecting them while travelling."

All at once Poppy dropped to her knees and started smoothing the reeds away from the hard-packed floor. As she knelt back on her heels they could all see the letters PERSEPH carved out.

"Could be a coincidence. Could have been 'ere months, sir," said Clarky.

"Quite true. Let's make ourselves presentable for dinner. They keep country hours here."

And with that Mr Gregory led them to the inn teasing John about losing one too many caps this year. There was a bounce in everyone's step as they walked away from the stable. Kitty took one last look behind and was sobered instantly. This was a lonely place despite the busy inn, no one would hear you cry. A child had been taken away from friends and family and she was becoming aware that she was having the time of her life, while Patrick was the one paying for it.

Supper had been quiet with Mr Gregory not joining them but spending the evening in the tap room, and Kitty decided on an early night for them all. Poppy was to sleep on a truck bed by the fire in her room with John next door. The reality was that while Poppy slept in her bed, Kitty wrapped herself in a shawl by the banked fire with a single candle and the Bible on her lap for company.

About six she could feel the inn coming to life, while the church bell and cries of the carriers leaving the town confirmed it was the start of another ordinary day. Kitty wondered if the men had found anything out last night and lack of proper sleep made her feel impatient that they hadn't seen fit to tell her anything.

She must have dozed as she was aware of Poppy with a tray of breakfast and a scullery maid carrying a jug of water and a fresh towel.

"Mr Gregory's compliments and asks that we be ready in half an hour. 'E found who stabled horses there and Mr Clark spoke to a lad who said that one of the horses was called Persephone and will be running at Epsom in three days. Come on, miss, we've gotta go!"

By the time she had changed, drank cooled coffee and nibbled at a piece of toasted bread before throwing it into the fire in disgust, Poppy was doing a jig in her impatience to be off. John had lost the dark bags under his eyes and was just as eager to be on the road. Kitty systematically checked both rooms for forgotten items and if the drawers and cupboards were not closed as quietly as they might have been, one look at her face forbade Poppy or John from commenting. The same look made Clarky beat a hasty retreat to the driving seat and Mr Gregory raise an eyebrow as he assisted her into the carriage. He followed Poppy and John inside and only then did she realise that his horse was tethered behind the carriage.

"Better to talk here than over breakfast," said Mr Gregory in explanation.

Yet nothing was said by Mr Gregory or Kitty until the last house of the town was passed. Kitty had come to a decision the previous night; this whole situation was not just irregular but wrong. John and Poppy thought it a lark and Lord alone knew what Mr Gregory thought as he never demeaned himself by sharing his thoughts with a mere governess! Then he went and surprised her:

"I had notice last night that Mr Bostock had recovered from his injuries and taken up a new post."

"What did you do?"

"Do?"

"To the curate, Mr Bostock. We know there were no burglars."

"No."

"So, what did you do?"

"Me?"

"Yes."

"Nothing."

"Nothing?"

"Nothing, I didn't lay a finger on him."

"And Mr Clark?"

"Not a finger."

"You are not going to tell me."

"I don't think you really want to know. But let me assure you his injuries were all of his own making."

It was not a conversation she was going to pursue in front of Poppy and John, so she lapsed into silence. After a few moments he continued: "I think that we should part company at the next post-house."

Even though this had been her exact thought, the fact that he had beaten her to airing it, raised her hackles.

"Just because—" But her indignant reply was drowned out by the exclamations, objections and arguments of her maid and her charge.

"I know that Miss Lucas will agree with me. This is not safe and to be frank you would be in the way." And this statement not only silenced Poppy but brought a deep blush to John's cheeks, who stammered out, "I am sorry to have been a burden, sir."

"Don't take offence, you'll return to Bath, where you are safe, and Miss Lucas and Poppy will go back to their lives which they have put aside to aid you young St John."

"I'm much obliged to them sir. But I wanted to help. To see it through."

"And just how do you see it ending? In a dramatic rescue of your friend and a triumphant return to school, where you'll be acclaimed a hero? Life rarely ends so neatly. We know little apart from the fact that Patrick was taken against his will and has not been seen since. We do not know where he is or why he was taken but what we do know is that the people we are dealing with hold life very cheap as you should know. They had no care whether you lived or died. Remember, we don't know whether you jumped or were pushed into the highway."

"That is sufficient, Mr Gregory. I think you have made your point." Kitty interrupted in the voice usually saved for high-spirited Sunday schoolers. "There is a small church coming up, I see. Let us pause and calm ourselves."

The order was given and the carriage pulled off the road. The men tended to the horses, while John, Kitty and Poppy wandered through the lychgate and into the well-tended graveyard. John strode off, with Poppy in pursuit. As she trod the small path, Kitty noticed the door to the church was ajar and wandered inside.

Two female parishioners were cleaning the lectern, so she slipped into a pew at the back and let out the breath she found she had been holding. She looked around the painted walls, dulled by age but depicting stories and struggles so familiar to her. This inevitably led to thoughts of her father and the realisation she had not thought of him in many days. The widows of the parish would be vying to organise his life the way she had. Why was she so unwilling to accept the life that had been designed for her?

She loved her father but she wanted more than being his housekeeper and then a spinster of the parish involved in everyone else's family but her own. Marriage was never a serious option. She had no dowry, while her looks and accomplishments were merely adequate. She had snatched at the role of governess but her family were unhappy with her decision. The compromise was being a companion to her aunt, but was this any different to being a companion to her father? Only time would tell.

She so wanted to have some control over her life, not for every decision to be made for her. She had almost made that first stand and it had been snatched from her by Mr Gregory. By now her anger had dissipated into self-pity. Recognising the emotion for what it was, she smiled at her own weakness, thanked God for putting up with her and left.

While the short break had stopped people saying some things they might regret, it didn't lead to agreement and Mr

Gregory took to riding alongside rather than inside the carriage. By midday they were in yet another stable yard waiting for horses to be changed. Kitty moved into the panelled interior of the house and ordered coffee, which was surprising good and accompanied by a rather fine slice of plum cake. Just as she was taking her third bite, a scraping of chair legs made her aware that she was no longer alone.

"This is where we part ways then, sir?" she said without looking.

"I have arranged for a driver to take you to Bath and return John to school. The account is paid for him then to return you and your maid to Epsom. I am much obliged for your good sense in all of this." And he pushed a bag of coin towards her. Ignoring the bag, she looked him directly in the eye. "Do you think you'll find him alive?"

"The body would have to be found in a very public manner for this all to have been worth the risk."

"Then you know the reason and the culprit."

"Yes."

"Then why on earth," she exclaimed, before continuing in more muted tones, "not just confront the man?"

"Do you not hunt, Miss Lucas?"

"I do not believe God gave us dominion over animals so that we could make sport of them, sir. No."

"Never make your prey desperate, Miss Lucas." And with that he stood, made his bow and left her.

Addressing herself to her cake, she added, "No, just make them exasperated."

When she returned to the carriage Mr Gregory and Clarky were nowhere in sight. She nodded at Poppy and John and smiled at the coachman.

"You are to take us to Bath and then Epsom…?"

"Timothy, ma'am. Yes, ma'am."

"Very well, but a slight change in order. First Epsom and then Bath."

Smiling at her two accomplices, she added, "Any objections?"

Poppy was the one who had objections. Kitty realised too late that for Poppy, Epsom meant a hard and stunted life as the young girl burst into tears sobbing out apologies for not being a proper abigail or for being too forward. It took all three of them to calm her.

Eventually they set off, having given Mr Gregory a good head start. Doing the calculations in her head and checking these with Timothy at the next stop, Kitty realised it would take two days to get there. Then what? Was there any point in them going?

She shared her thoughts with Poppy and John over supper.

"Mr Gregory never goes straight at a problem. The Races start in three days with lots of comings and goings and accidents, if you catch my drift.

Uneducated Poppy might be, but she was not unintelligent and she had been thinking too.

"I don't think we should go straight to Epsom anyways. Cos the men that took John could be there and …"

"And you don't want your father seeing you, either," he countered.

"You're both right. Which has given me an idea…"

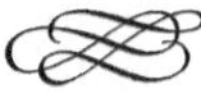

When Kitty's eyes flickered open she felt no pain, just a numbness in her legs. But as she blinked and realised that the gloom was not dissipating her head began to throb. Her throat was dry and the smell which reached her finally was astringent but stale. She felt strangely calm however. The plan didn't seem to have worked. But something was missing, or rather someone and with that thought she slept.

A cold light and even colder draught wakened her a second time. Again, her eyes closed.

The third time she woke the night was giving way to the dawn and she was leaning against an aged hay bale. Someone grumbled in their sleep. How had she got here? In response her memory returned.

Her initial idea had been to find an inn not too far from Tadworth, and Timothy suggested the Duke's Head as being suitable. The plan was to lie low and scout out the area near the racecourse where Patrick may be hidden. Poppy was to ask around the yard while John and Kitty pretended to be interested in old churches

"And if someone recognises me then they'll have to act," announced John. That was not unforeseen but not her intention at all and even Mr Gregory had baulked at having the boy as bait. She would have to keep him on a short leash.

What Kitty didn't share was the idea which had grown from the seed Mr Gregory had sown. There had been no ransom for Patrick or demands of any kind. John had been left for dead. If his death was Patrick's fate why did they not kill him immediately. Why wait? Why move him? And why towards Epsom? Accidents happened in crowds. But this was April and the beginning of the spring season – so huge crowds of people seemed unlikely. They just had to look, methodically. They would start with the area around the racecourse and work out.

The plan seemed fine and not at all influenced by the novels her friends read. She of course never read them but did enjoy the snippets copied in letters from the girls she had known at school. The fact that there was no money for such frippery, well for a frippery so disapproved of by her father, was incidental. Oh dear, her mind was wandering.

They had been very jolly on their journey to Epsom; a bunch of truants enjoying the freedom. But once ensconced in the inn recommended by Timothy, located slightly off the beaten track, their mood quietened. Fortified by an excellent meal of cold ham, chicken and cheese they pooled their knowledge.

Mr Gregory's plan to return them to the safety of Bath, assumed that Epsom and its environs must be dangerous. They had one potential lead, Persephone. Poppy was sent to the kitchen to find out what she could. Meanwhile, Kitty's thoughts raced: Patrick must be hidden somewhere and they must find where.

Mrs Wellings was their hostess. Kitty needed her as an ally, so tackling her through compliments seemed a good start.

"That was excellent cheese, Mrs Wellings."

"Well thank you miss, my old gran taught me and I've always kept my hand in. Not many of the gentry care for sheep's cheese these days."

John excused himself and left for the stables. Mrs Wellings seemed a valuable soul and would only need a little encouragement.

"My father swore by it for building up strength and my charge is still not fully recovered. The journey has been hard on him so I thought a couple of days in one place exploring the area would be good. However, I think churches hold little interest for him. Are there any ruins or battlefields nearby?"

"Not really miss. I would think the racecourse would be of interest."

"I think you are probably right. But I know nothing of them and I do not know whether his guardian would think it educational enough. I am sure there are many fine houses in the area, but again I do not think they would pique his interest."

"He does look rather bruised. If it's not an impertinence, what happened?"

"I am not sure of the details but it resulted in a rather serious fall and the last thing I want is for him to get into another scrape."

Mrs Wellings looked thoughtful. "How about haunted houses?"

"Well…" Kitty feigned indifference.

"Not that I believe in such nonsense, of course. But I was thinking of the boy."

This sounded promising, what better place to hide someone than in a place no one would look, but successful fishing needed a fine hand. Kitty adjusted her seat to look at the landlady. She was round. Her eyes were a dimmed blue, her cheeks rosy and lips full. Her once fair hair was also faded but she had a friendly open face. She must have been pretty when young and while now dulled, Kitty could see that her temperament was kind and her hands and expertly patched apron showed that she was hardworking.

Mr Wellings had found a good match and in response he had not given her any major trouble. Her weakness lay in needing to know all that went on and she probably prided herself on this. Kitty smiled:

"As long as the building was structurally sound, I think you may well have hit on the very thing!"

As soon as the good dame departed Poppy appeared with, "Aw miss, I thought the old trout would never leave."

"Poppy, we really do need to speak about your language if you are going to make the move from the scullery,"

"Yeh, but not now, eh? I found him!"

"Who? Patrick?"

"Nah…"

"Poppy!" interrupted Kitty, "Really."

"No miss, I mean," Poppy enunciated clearly before continuing in a babble, "That Hughes-Templeton fella."

"Mr Templeton-Hughes," enunciated Kitty. "You mean Patrick's uncle?"

"Reverend Templeton-Hughes up at Langley," corrected Poppy.

"Now that, Poppy, is very interesting indeed."

Timothy drove them to Langley churchyard and arranged to collect them from the White Swan at the other end of the village. Poppy took her role as Abigail and spy very seriously, which surprised both her companions.

In order to wheedle information from their host, not only did Poppy want to mend the rip in a brown pelisse but she had also persuaded Mrs Wellings to show her how to make a special posset lauded through the ages by Mrs Wellings's ancestors as a sure way to bring bodies back to a fine fettle. John looked concerned and truculent in equal measure when he discovered this.

Mrs Wellings also made mention that today was market day, which meant the party could keep their ears and eyes open while hiding among the crowds.

Having received a full description of the area, Kitty decided that starting at the churchyard and then wandering aimlessly around the village would mark them as curious tourists rather than seekers after truth.

The church was quite pretty and the graveyard neat though some of the older plots needed some attention.

Far across the fields she could see men walking the racecourse, though it was still weeks to the first races. She knew that part of the puzzle lay with the race but that part she didn't feel capable of addressing – and that she felt was where Mr Gregory would have his sights set.

This town was sure to be packed with locals and visitors from London when it came to June.

The image of Mr Gregory would not be banished from Kitty's mind. She had never been one to be courted and, to be fair, she had always discouraged any flirting. It made her uncomfortable and she found it dishonest; as the men she would have been suited to wed needed a dowry and those who did not desired someone more vivacious and, to be blunt, pretty.

So it was that she was unaccustomed to making conversation. True, she could converse with her father's friends about theology and the classics, make small talk with confirmed spinsters of the parish and give advice to her friends from childhood, but talking to members of the Ton was a skill she did not possess and had no need for. So why did she wish she had attained it? Would it make him see her in a different light? Did she want him to? She would be lying to herself if she said no. He had worked his way very much into her thoughts and she knew herself well enough to know that finding Patrick was not the only motive for this search.

After spending a decent amount of time in the graveyard they meandered towards the river and followed it past the old oak. Mrs Wellings was very well informed. Poking out from behind the trees was an old wooden structure. Dark, but with the roof intact, this was the mill-house that popular rumour said was haunted.

As they approached across the sheep-cropped grass they saw that the windows were boarded over and the mill race ran free with rotting paddles from the old wheel discarded on the side of the track leading from the road. Yet Kitty noticed that the track itself was clear and that the main entry doors, previously used for carts to enter fully laden, looked solid. Laying a hand on John's sleeve they stopped and listened. Birds could be heard in the trees above, crows by the sound of them and though somewhat subdued by their approach, they continued their arguments in the still bare branches above them. Though a mere stone's throw from the village this was a quiet and secluded spot.

From the stones and bricks in the hedgerows the village had been larger at one time and it looked as if the mill had continued to ply its trade until quite recently. Curious as to how a mill could become unused - everyone needed flour - Kitty looked at the water course. Little more than a trickle of water ran sluggishly in the deep cut, indicating that at one time the water would have been faster and more abundant.

"As you can see, the water would have been drawn into the mill and used to power a range of machinery…"

"Miss Lucas who are you talking to?"

Smiling she turned towards John and adding *sotto voce*, "We don't know if anyone is watching." Then she continued at her previous volume, "So what were such mills used for in this part of the world?"

"Would it be flour? Do you think there is any machinery left?" And staying in role he raced over to the main entrance followed by his ever-patient governess. Or that was the impression Kitty hoped they gave although, to her ears, it sounded wooden and forced.

As she had deduced from a distance, the doors were solid and well-maintained. Running her finger over the hinges gave her glove a sheen of fresh oil and there was a significant lock in place.

"Oh please, Mr Francis, do not go racing off again, whatever will I say to your mother?" All the while shooing him away with both hands. Eventually John took the hint, laughed and raced off. She stood stock still and listening hard for any internal sounds. Livestock maybe or a frightened boy? There was nothing. If this was a novel she would be sadly disappointed.

All at once she became aware of a noise behind her; a rider obscured by the trees. She turned hoping John would stay out of sight until the unwelcome visitor had left. Adopting what she hoped was the facial expression of an exasperated governess she waited until the rider came into view proper.

"Mr Francis, are you there? The owner is coming and will not take kindly to your trespassing."

With smile in place she turned to face the rider. The Welsh cob was a stocky creature but carried his rider like a bag of potatoes. Not a natural rider, she thought. The man was dressed in breeches and a jerkin worn, washed and mended many times. His boots were strong and again showed excellent care. But, as he came closer, his face did not exhibit the friendliest of countenances and it became seriously severe as he looked over her shoulder.

Turning, she saw that John had either not heard or headed her warning.

"Miss Lucas. Look th..."

"Oi, what you two doing 'ere. 'S private property!"

Taking a step forward, Kitty replied in full governess manner, "We realise that now, sir. We thought it a ruin when we spied it from the church. My apologies and I can assure you that we meant and have done no harm."

Slightly mollified, the rider slid from rather than dismounted his horse, "Well, you never can be too careful." His leg became hung on a sack part way down and a certain undignified wriggling was required. Kitty glowered at John daring him to snigger while presenting the man with a perfectly passive face.

Deciding to risk her arm, she countered with, "Perhaps you could give us some information about the structure. I thought it had perhaps been a water mill?"

"It was miss, but maister uses it for storing stuff these days. I used to work 'ere when I was a lad. You can still see sluice gates..."

He wandered in the direction of the ruined race with Kitty in tow. She nodded to John towards the sacks on the horse.

"...there was a time when this mill worked day and night. But the new mill works just as well and is nearer the new road. When all was enclosed it changed things you see, miss."

Kitty had often heard the old farm hands in her neck of the woods decrying the Enclosure Acts. It was a more efficient way of farming but many lost out when the common lands and historic rights could not be documented or proved.

"Who owns the land around here?"

"Mostly the Templetons but the Brierleys have a good chunk too. This 'ere belongs to the parson, though he's related."

"Is the church there his?"

"Aye. Though he won't be holding services since he broke

his leg. Old Canon Greaves will probably step in. Likes to keep his hand in, like."

"Well, thank you for the information on the mill. I hope I haven't held you up too much. We best be getting on now. Come along J… Mr Francis."

Inclining her head and reminding John to make his salute then began to retrace their steps towards the church. She shushed him with inconsequential chatter about spring flowers and the importance of a flood plain until they were well out of earshot.

Bending to examine an imaginary flower, she started with, "Well what was in the sack?"

"His nuncheon – milk, pie, bread, lump of cheese and an apple! Do you think we could have something before we head back?"

"More than likely. Maybe Poppy has had more luck. The mill didn't seem very haunted to me."

"Oh, that reminds me. I found a door in the ground. A trapdoor thing it opened into a thin tunnel. I was coming to tell you when the man appeared."

"Milk?"

"What?"

"Pardon is the word. Milk! Did he have milk?"

"Well, yes. Why?"

"I have never met a working man who went off to work with milk. Cider, beer, water even but not milk!"

"What do we do?"

"Right now, we need Timothy."

With that they continued their route past the church and along the road to the White Swan.

They found Timothy checking one of the horse's hooves with another man. They both doffed their headgear as she appeared.

"Sorry miss, but this one's shoes loose."

"Can it be repaired?"

"Yes miss, but best done properly. Farrier's in back and can get it done now if we don't mind waiting a bit."

"How long is a bit?"

"About an hour he says."

"That would be satisfactory. A small repast for the ever-hungry amongst us and then evensong."

John smiled and then groaned.

"Can you collect us from the church?"

Replete with cold pork pie and a small glass of cider, they were soon on their way back to the church. Halfway there and the bell summoned the tardier to prayers. Never the most popular of services, it was always one of Kitty's favourite. There wasn't the expectation of the sermon or communion but a comforting end to the day, a time to give thanks and take comfort in familiar hymns and responses.

After the service an elderly man led the congregation from the church, standing at the door to give his blessing to their journey home. Kitty and John held back a little on the pretence of looking for her glove. From the snippets of conversation she heard, she discovered that this was the elderly Canon Greaves.

"Thank you, Canon," said Kitty taking the proffered hand.

"Lovely to see new faces. Are you staying locally?"

"No, just visiting and was enchanted by the church. Is that your vicarage next door?"

"Yes, it is the vicarage, dear lady. But no longer mine, I am merely holding the fort so to speak. Reverend Templeton-Hughes is the incumbent here."

"Ah yes, I remember hearing of him. Hasn't he a son at school in Bath?"

"On no, his son is a man of the world now. Often comes to visit."

Smiling she and John moved on to allow two elderly ladies

access. However, the road was empty of Timothy and their carriage.

"It looks like the horse is not quite shod. Let's take a final look at that mill."

The afternoon had ended in cloud and the light was beginning to fade more quickly than Kitty had thought. They walked in silence to the mill and she began to question the sanity of what she was doing and in fact had been doing all day. She was charged with looking after a boy who had very nearly died and here she was walking him towards a mill which could be haunted, dangerous or worse. And why? Simply because she was piqued. Governess was definitely not her calling if her base impulses put a child at risk.

Yet while she was admonishing herself inwardly, she kept on walking, conscious of a stir of excitement and contentment.

As they drew nearer the barn they lessened their pace and sought the cover of the hedgerow as they scuttled around the back of the barn to the trapdoor John had discovered. They couldn't tell if the man was still there, and they didn't have a good tale to tell if he was.

John had rushed ahead and as he re-appeared he started to speak then his face went ash grey. Instinctively, she turned on her heel and came face to face with a small mountain of a man. Automatically she took a step back and lost her footing in the long grass and began to slide away from her would-be captor into a hidden cutting.

However, she felt herself saved by her assailant grabbing her dress and hauling her back onto firm ground. Any self-respecting maiden in distress would had swooned gracefully. This was not Kitty's way and she kicked out like a harridan, telling when she had made contact by the oaths emitting from her captor. His hand was over her nose and mouth and soon her struggles became weaker, she could sense rather than see John entering into the fray but it was a hopeless case.

"John, John. Are you awake?" stunned by the banality of the question she felt her way towards the sleeper, trying to avoid thinking about the occasional soft patch of straw she crawled over.

"Oh, thank goodness, Miss Lucas, I was really scared," said a voice from behind her.

"John? So who's this?"

She had reached the inert but snoring body in front of her.

"It's Patrick, Miss Lucas. We found him."

Her eyes were becoming more attuned to the gloom and she could see John step towards the boy shaking him unceremoniously. She could make out eaves shrouded in dust and cobwebs as the light of a grey dawn gingerly made its way through slits and gaps in the roof.

In the twilight she determined the location of the sleeper's shoulder and shook it hard. "Wake up, Patrick." He groaned and stretched.

Kitty turned back to John. "What happened yester'eve?"

"One of the men who took us. We recognised each other at the same moment. You really should have kept cave, you know!"

"I ... yes I should. I beg your pardon, I gather we are in the mill. Any ideas on how to get out?"

"No, but now you're awake I think we should be going. Come on, Patrick."

The somnolent Patrick was waking, though noisily and in gradual stages. Kitty was aware of both relief and fear in John's tone and the urgency of their case was obvious. Plans had been laid which her actions had overturned, whatever fate was in store for Patrick would now be shared by them too. Unbidden, Mr Gregory's advice never to make your prey desperate came to mind.

Once Patrick seemed fully awake introductions were made. He was both delighted and horrified that his friend was here, but in the same predicament. Kitty took charge.

"Patrick, look for trapdoors. John, test all the window coverings."

She stood, brushed goodness knows what from her clothing and tried to get her bearings.

"How long was I asleep?"

"It went dark and now it's not..." was all the information to be obtained from John happy to have something to do. Timothy would have waited at the church, but for how long? And then what?

"I think I have something, miss," said a quiet voice. Patrick sounded weak and maybe drugged. She stepped quickly to his side. He was clammy to the touch and was shivering slightly. She squeezed his shoulder for encouragement and saw an old ring attached to the wooden floor. It turned, but it took mutual effort to pull it open. A dank smell suggested that this gave access to the race and as such was not a first choice for an escape route. But maybe it connected to the door John had found?

They were all now looking for an exit but the door was solid and heavy and most of the windows were too high. It looked like machinery had been removed and the area was now used only for storage. There were some cases around and flattened areas suggested that more boxes may be found here at different times. Though Kitty couldn't tell what the boxes might have contained in this light, she felt around and found a fibrous material she supposed was used for packing. A convoluted link took her thoughts to those of Poppy. Would she have raised the alarm or covered for them?

The boys were both testing the wall at the far end, so the scraping noises Kitty heard were not them. Rats maybe? But this sounded like a tattoo rather than hungry gnawing and was coming from the door. Cautiously she moved towards it. There were voices. Anxiously she moved closer.

"Well they've got to be somewhere."

A mumbled reply didn't make it through the door.

"You got a better idea then? Thought not!" The voice was recognisable now.

"Poppy. We're here. Can you get us out?" Kitty shouted.

As it transpired, the answer was no. Neither of the rescuers was proficient at breaking or picking locks nor had they had the forethought to bring any tools with them. The dawn was becoming more insistent and the time had come to face the trapdoor solution.

Kitty and John managed the door between them but Patrick was almost in a trance. Kitty was more and more convinced that he had been drugged.

"John, did you have any of the milk?"

"Would have done if there was any left. I'm parched now."

Shafts of light pierced the gloom. Kitty glimpsed the empty milk pail, no help there.

"Timothy, where is the carriage?"

"Here, miss."

"Be ready to move the moment we get to you and drive away from the vicarage not past it."

And with that she motioned for John to go first. She helped Patrick down into the shaft which was about seven feet deep and felt John take his weight. She followed, pulling the door shut behind her. The blackness was absolute she felt a moment of fear. As she adjusted and tried not to breathe in the stench, part of her was extremely relieved they couldn't see what they were stepping on. The tunnel was clay-lined and after about 20 yards John came upon two steps.

"Can you hold Patrick while I see what's here?"

Feeling with his hands and feet he moved up, she realised that she could see his shape – light was coming in from somewhere then. Luck was certainly on their side the access door was poorly maintained with no lock, and they were soon up in the open air. Now for the carriage.

Poppy was exultant, hopping from one foot to another as she held the door and step. Timothy had the horses in hand and ready for the off. Bundling the children in she told all of them to lie on the floor. On pure intuition, she ensured the blinds were up so any observer would see nothing inside, then she lay down too.

"Not a sound, anyone," she whispered and only slightly louder, "Take us back Timothy, but sedately. Act as if you have no passengers."

Kitty expected them to be hauled over at any time. Why was there no guard on the mill? What was the injured vicar doing? What story would she have for Mrs Wellings? Did she have to go back to the inn or should they make straight for Bath?

"We're coming up to the toll, miss. What do you want to do?"

Kitty thought fast. If anyone was pursuing them they'd ask the turnpike. Hoisting herself and Poppy onto the seats she prepared to look like a respectable young lady in a carriage albeit at a very unusual hour.

"Poppy, how far are we from your home?"

"Not sure, miss. Why? If you're thinking we'd find a welcome there you'd be mistaken. Too many mouths to feed to welcome more."

"Anyone with less mouths to feed that might help? We need to clean up and Patrick is not well."

"There's nan, but she lives in an alms house at St George's so we'd stand out like a sore thumb. She was cook for Mr Robertson until…"

Her voice trailed off and a curious gleam came to her eye.

Mr Robertson's country seat consisted of a small hunting lodge inherited from his godmother. When he had married three years previously his new bride took one look and moved the entire establishment to Bath and there they stayed. Nan had been retired and the place left empty.

Kitty was sure that Timothy would think that this far outreached his contract of hire. But in this she had underestimated Poppy. Not only had she persuaded him to return to the mill rather than raise the alarm but he calmly acquiesced to the change in route. Poppy stayed atop to help with directions leaving Kitty and her two schoolboys.

It was a subdued party that drew into the stables at the Robertson's. While Timothy tended to the horses, Poppy retraced the steps of her younger self finding the backdoor key mid the rampant mint in the kitchen garden.

They had soon set up camp in the kitchen. It was dry and dusty. The broken pantry window from a winter storm was strangely comforting. As it hadn't been mended it meant that no one visited regularly to keep an eye on the place. It was cold but Kitty did not want to risk signs of habitation by starting a fire. They placed Patrick in the warmer east-facing parlour where he was soon asleep. With a curious collection of honey and preserved fruits foraged from the backs of cupboards to sustain them, they began to plan.

Timothy's contribution was to agree with whatever Poppy said. Poppy thought they needed to find Mr Gregory as soon as possible.

"And just where would you start?"

"At stables in Epsom, miss. 'E was on the tail of that mare Persephone."

"And the boys? Patrick is hardly in a fit condition and John is barely mended from his last encounter. We still don't know who we're up against or why."

After a few minutes Kitty found herself only half-listening to Poppy who was excited and egged on by her new swain's attention. The situation had suddenly come home to Kitty as a gnawing hole in the pit of her stomach that, though she had perhaps indeed saved Patrick in the short term, she had undoubtedly put all of them in a very precarious position.

Standing, she brushed remnants of straw and sticks from her gown.

"It is late or early. Let us get a little rest and then decide."

Timothy went to sleep with his horses while the boys took a chaise and trestle respectively while Poppy made herself at home with some dust covers, a garish rug and her cloak.

Kitty watched as the day delivered bright sunshine initially before seasonally tipping its toe back into winter with a quick flurry of snow, then settling on a more sensible light drizzle. All this while her mind flitted between the facts.

She had realised quite quickly that whole chunks of the puzzle were missing. Innocent to an incredible degree, she had gone along with everything Mr Gregory had said, and indeed had asked of her, without question. Why? Because he was well-dressed and exuded confidence? Well yes. But surely Dr Parkin would not be so easily swayed? What power did Edward Gregory have to act at all? Why was he involving himself in the fate of unimportant schoolboys?

The only people who she felt she could trust were Dr Parkin and Mrs Titherington. She had made a decision. This was England. She was a governess. She was taking her charges back to school in Bath. There were no cutthroats waiting to interrupt them on their legitimate business.

She roused Kitty after a couple of hours and sent her to get some water and cloths for washing. It would be a cold wash but her charges needed to look presentable. Covering her head against the drizzle she found Timothy talking to his horses while grooming them.

"I want to leave within the hour and get as far as we can towards Bath. Where do you think we can reach tonight?"

"Could get to the other side of Leatherhead, miss, if the weather brightens. You won't be wantin' to travel in the dark?"

"That would be marvellous." And with that she returned to the house and started to search the bedrooms for clothes. Luckily, the Robertson's had left clothes behind and, though not the height of fashion, she managed to ensure the boys had clean presentable clothing. With Poppy's assistance she was able to freshen some parts of her apparel with a mish-mash of petticoats, linen shirts and cloak. There was even an ugly bonnet which helped her look rather more the part.

Before they departed, Kitty sent Poppy and John to the upper floors to find trunks and fill them with a mixture of clothes and linens. John made to question her, but she forestalled him with:

"Visitors at inns without trunks and boxes invite questions."

Then she turned to Patrick.

"How are you feeling today?"

"Much better, miss. Thank you. How did you and John find me?"

"To be honest, luck. What can you remember?"

"Well I remember being grabbed and a sack put over my head. After that it was a bit foggy. I was given something strong and spicy to drink and I slept a lot. I think John was there to start with but then another man came and they talked about horses and one of them went away. I was a bit more awake after that."

"Did you recognise the man?"

"No. He only came once. Normally it was two men with rough hands. They talked about horses a lot but just picked me up and took me to places… stables I think and then the barn."

"Do you remember writing something on the floor?"

"On yes, Persephone. They kept on going on about it. I'd had some bread and porridge and was feeling a bit brighter so I used a bit of stone to write the name. You found it?"

"Yes, we found it. You did well."

The roads were good in this part of the country and, since the weather and time of year kept people at home, they made good time. They changed horses in Leatherhead and to watch their coin Poppy was sent shopping for bread, cooked meat, cheese and milk. With the progress and food, their spirits rose and John started to explain that he had found a kitten … They were soon comparing notes on school and on what they would have to do when they returned, but Kitty noted how they both stayed away from their more recent experiences.

Kitty felt herself on tenterhooks the whole way to Bath, every mile of the way she felt they might be overhauled and caught. With careful driving and changing of horses they made good time and aimed for busy well-used inns. They achieved it within three days in total without incident. Kitty always had Poppy or Timothy ask of the ostlers if anything had been seen of Mr Gregory or Clarky but nothing came of it. What could they be doing?

It was a wet Wednesday. Kitty found herself back in Bathwick Hall amidst exclamations, questions and profuse expressions of gratitude. Mrs Titherington ushered Poppy, Patrick and John away, while Kitty was left in the cosy library with Dr Parkin.

"Mr Gregory is not with you, my dear?"

"No, we parted company near Epsom and he charged me with returning John. It was sheer luck we happened upon Patrick."

"Umm in a barn? How on earth did he get there?"

"I am not sure of the sequence of events and I do not think Patrick is any the wiser either. He appears to have been drugged for the majority of the episode."

"Boys are remarkable beasts. I expect to hear exaggerated highlights of daring do within about a week."

"I certainly do hope so."

After supper, Kitty found herself in splendid isolation in a clean, warm room which wasn't accompanied by sounds from the tap room or from the stable, or indeed from the thought of the rightful owners returning at any minute. She felt herself give way to the silence as a long sigh escaped and her shoulders relaxed.

Slipping between warmed sheets she welcomed a deep and refreshing sleep but it refused to come. She turned the pillow to find a cool side. She lit the candle. She sipped water. Finally, she slipped on a robe and went to sit by the window, squeezing herself between the curtain and the windowpane and watched the moon and clouds make sport with the shadows in the gardens beneath her.

All the time she turned over events, posed questions, eliminated hypotheses and eventually came to the conclusion that she needed to know the why. Why these boys had been taken was the key to the whole thing.

# TAKING NOTHING AT FACE VALUE

*A*lthough Kitty enjoyed an exciting story of treachery and romance she did not believe that these gave a true or useful blueprint for solving mysteries. Closer inspection of reports from the criminal court might have served her better, but when she did pay attention to her father's newspaper she was usually more concerned with the court circular. Her most useful experience to draw upon had to be Uncle Stuart, who presided over the assizes. A friend of her father's since they were boys he would often discuss cases over dinner, neither men thinking of the suitability of the topic before a young girl not yet out. The information that this gave Kitty was that most crimes were rooted in power or money.

They had not started out to kill John; he was just not wanted. His death would be convenient as it covered the mistake in taking him. Patrick was the real target as he had not been disposed of. Instead, he had been restrained until the right time. Patrick was too young for power so money had to be the key. He was an orphan. In stories, the evil stepmother or wicked uncle were the villain, but in real-life? Kitty had to know more and she had an idea on how to accomplish this.

Wearied by her mental exercises, a yawn escaped her, so untucking her feet, she padded back to the bed and entered a deep sleep.

After two days of recuperation, Kitty became restless. She should be making plans for her trip to London or at least earning her lodgings. Yet there was something that restrained her, she did not feel the game was over and certainly did not feel that Patrick was safe despite the authorities being informed.

Those feelings were accentuated when Dr Parkin opened his letter over breakfast. Mrs Titherington and Dr Parkin enjoyed a family-style meal in the mornings as a way of discussing the day's plans and as a respite at the beginning of the day from the needs of children and their masters. Kitty noticed that the letter was of heavy paper – a waste of money in her eyes – and written in a florid hand. The contents must not have been fulfilling as she noticed Dr Parkin turning the sheet over looking for more.

"I believe we should expect a visitor later on today - Patrick's guardian, Reverend Templeton-Hughes."

"Well, it is only to be expected," soothed Mrs Titherington, "He will be concerned over the boy's welfare. I am sure that when he sees that Patrick is fighting fit, he will be comforted."

"Did someone mention that he had injured his leg?" Kitty controlled the concern in her voice and knew that this control needed to be extended to her and the boy's conduct too. She had kept her exploits and suppositions to herself but what would she do if he wanted to take his ward away? Aunt Caroline's voice sounded in her ear: *Cross that bridge when you come to it, my dear.*

"Unfortunately, I believe he was thrown from his horse. I am glad to hear that he is now well enough to travel."

"Though of course he may be visiting Bath for medical

reasons too," added Mrs Titherington. "He has never overly concerned himself with Patrick's wellbeing before now. Yet these have been most unusual occurrences." And with that she stood, smoothed down her apron, adjusted the keys at her waist, and started her day.

"Dr Parkin," said Kitty. "I feel that now Patrick is settled and his guardian due, that I should continue with my original plan to join my aunt in London. Where should I find the booking office?"

Although the good man made the expected remarks of her always being welcome, and that she should not rush her plans, Kitty and Dr Parkin knew that the time was right. So, with directions written on a piece of pasteboard, pelisse and hat in place and finally Poppy in tow, they set off for the centre of good taste and high gossip – Bath.

It was certainly a pretty place. The buildings were elegant and the people matched them with polished canes and the most amazing lace. She was most smitten with the hats. The glorious plumes and range of colours and sizes intrigued her. However, the directions Dr Parkin had given her, and Mrs Titherington had amended for a more direct route, took her off the main thoroughfare through neat but constrained architecture and finally to the merely functional. Here the calm elegant stroll was replaced by the hustle and bustle of people whose energy and work kept them out of poverty.

With tickets purchased for the day after tomorrow, Kitty returned to the main town with a silent Poppy in place. Though a little surprised by Poppy's reticence at the sight of such finery and the idea of travelling as far as London, Kitty did not press the matter. Timothy had left with his carriage the day after their arrival in Bath, while John and Patrick, reunited, were inseparable and threw themselves into school life. All of this left Poppy bereft and lonely. Mrs Titherington had seen this and her answer was to give the girl plenty to do, but this just emphasised the gap between her and John. Kindly meant in the long and short-term, it was a cruel solution.

Dr Parkin's original instructions had taken Kitty past the baths with notes on what Roman features to look out for, so following these Kitty prepared herself to play the blue-stocking-cum-country-bumpkin, amazed by her surroundings and interested in the architecture and history.

They returned footsore and weary, but Kitty felt pleased to have indulged herself in her freedom – something she had not done since her stroll around Epsom, which seemed like months ago. Likewise, Poppy had enjoyed a day off from the usual chores.

A rather nice carriage with a sombre-clad driver was waiting outside the school. It was dusty and a little smeared with mud which indicated a long-distance traveller. Was this the elusive Reverend? Pre-warned and prepared, Kitty advanced toward the library.

"Oh, my apologies Dr Parkin, I did not realise that you were entertaining?" Kitty feigned fluster and prepared to leave.

"A welcome interruption, dear Miss Lucas, allow me to introduce the Reverend Templeton-Hughes."

The reverend gentleman inclined his head and smiled as Kitty made her curtsy. "Please excuse me not standing Miss Lucas, my leg pains me a great deal and the journey was a little more tiring than I had anticipated."

The breeches, stocking and buckles would not have been out of place in a portrait of a revered reverend from the old King's days. His thin frame supported a rotund middle which spoke of good dinners and insufficient exercise. Despite the crotchetiness of his responses, smile lines were hidden in the wrinkles but the smile never quite made it to his lines. Charming but cold was her judgement. A typical unmarried cleric and not the best guardian for an adventurous boy.

Kitty took the chair to one side as indicated by Dr Parkin whose fixed grin warned Kitty that all had not been pleasantries before her entrance.

"I hope you find Patrick no worse for his adventures, sir."

"A little more subdued and I think the event may play on his mind for some time to come. I must thank you for your part in his return."

"A sheer fluke sir, I assure you. I am just glad that no irreparable damage was done and that he could be restored to his friends. Boys are most resilient when surrounded by their peers, I find."

"You have much experience of young boys, Miss Lucas?"

"Oh yes, did not Dr Parkin explain, I am a governess."The Reverend raised an eyebrow: "You look quite young for such an undertaking."

"How kind of you to say, sir. And may I enquire what are your plans for Patrick now?"

"Dr Parkin and were discussing that just now as you entered."

Smiling Kitty rose, "Then I will leave you to your discussions." With that she made her bow and left and went in search of Mrs Titherington.

She found the good lady counting bedsheets. "You know, Miss Lucas, I have no idea what boys do with bedsheets." Holding one up with a hole in the middle she added, "though perhaps that is for the best." She put down the sheet. "Did you find the offices easily enough?"

"Yes, thank you. I have booked seats for myself and Poppy. I just need to impose on your hospitality for two more nights."

"It is no imposition. Though Reverend Templeton-Hughes deciding that this is the best place to rest his leg tonight, might well be." With that she returned to the laundry.

Thoughtfully, Kitty returned to her room to be met by a deputation of boys and Poppy. As she expected, Patrick and

John were there, but so were four others all looking stern and not a little excited. Not a good combination in her experience.

"Gentlemen?"

With the accompanying raised eyebrow, the sternness melted to concern and the excitement was a little quelled.

"Miss Lucas, what are we to do? My uncle wants me to return with him. He says he can keep me safe and Dr Parkin can't. It's boring. I'll run away."

"He'll do for 'im," said a large solid young man.

"All we did to get him back. It will have all been for nothing," added John.

"I gather that nothing has been decided. Dr Parkin and your uncle are still talking. At the end of the day, he is your guardian," answered Kitty. "We must do nothing rash."

"But, Miss Lucas …" said the boys in unison.

"What do you expect me to do? Whisk you away? Forbid him contact? Neither of those options is in my arsenal. We can try to manoeuvre your uncle to our way of thinking but we must be subtle. Do you understand?"

Reluctantly the boys nodded and Poppy pursed her lips and crossed her arms.

Kitty leaned in closer and the boys gathered round. "Now, Patrick, you have a reputation for being adventurous. We could try using that but then if we go too far your uncle may just bring in a tutor skilled in dealing with such behaviour. What we want is for you to stay here and, above all, stay safe. But we don't really know from what or why, so we are at a disadvantage. Maybe we would obtain more information through kindness and acquiescence?"

The looks and mutterings from the band of seven warriors she took for compliance if not agreement.

"Nothing will happen tonight. Your uncle is staying here and tomorrow is another day. Keep Patrick in sight at all times if you want to help him. Poppy, you keep an ear out to what is said by the servants. Perhaps we could share information after breakfast tomorrow?"


Dinner was a pleasant and quiet affair just comprising of Dr Parkin, Mrs Titherington, the Reverend and Kitty. The boys ate separately for which Kitty was grateful as they could have said either too much or too little. She was at a loss to know how to continue with this game and wished, not for the first time, since Langley that Mr Gregory was there. What was he up to?

Kitty re-focussed on the conversation around her and found that Mr Templeton-Hughes was talking about his brother – Patrick's father.

"Yes, he was definitely the older brother and I was always in awe of him. To me, he always knew the right thing to say and could smooth away problems with a smile. He was a huge favourite with the old king and was said to have significant influence at court. It was the travelling between Hanover and London that was his undoing as he and his wife faced one storm too many and all hands were lost."

There was little to say apart from acknowledgements and commiserations from the other dinners. Dr Parkin attempted to lighten the mood.

"I believe your parish is very close to Epsom – does the racing affect the area greatly?"

"Certainly, and for good and ill. There is employment, which is welcome, but unsavoury types are drawn to the area who lead the young and impetuous astray. However, the skill of the riders fascinates me. I believe I had made something of a science of the techniques involved. The ability to place the beast and then to attune oneself to the creature's rhythms is almost spiritual. Add to this the tactics and strategy of a general to pace the beast and to position oneself to strike at the most opportune time. Then there is the throb and vibrations of the hooves finding good ground from bad.

He had become quite animated and there was a flush about his cheeks and a faraway look in his eyes which to Kitty's eyes did not sit well with his chosen profession. As if reading her mind, he added. "But my calling took me away from the track not onto it."

After his impassioned speech, Mr Templeton-Hughes declined the sweet course and bade them goodnight, giving the excuse of pain in his leg and a need for a good night's sleep if he was to attempt the journey tomorrow. After wishing him a restorative night and waiting for his stick to make its way down the corridor, Kitty turned to her hosts:

"It is settled then? They leave tomorrow?"

"I have not spoken to Patrick, but yes,' the doctor replied, somewhat forlorn. 'His uncle is understandably concerned about his kidnapping and asked me for reassurance that his nephew would be safe from any and all harm. That is a something I cannot give."

"But nobody could, Dr Parkin, not even his own uncle."

"Of course not. But the events brought home to him the pain of his brother's death and the thought of losing the only remaining connection to him is very painful to the good Reverend."

"My dear," enquired Mrs Titherington, "You seem distressed, do you know something about Patrick's kidnapping that you are not telling us?"

"Nothing I know for certain but definitely suspicions. Is Patrick well-provided for?"

"Oh certainly, there is quite a large inheritance from both his mother and father with him being an only child. What are you suggesting?" asked Dr Parkin. "Surely this was merely an opportunist crime not thought through."

"Probably something highly slanderous, sir, so please pay me no mind. I think the events of the last few weeks have heightened my susceptibility to melodrama."

Mr Templeton-Hughes took his breakfast in his room, and with no further chance of obtaining information or anything else, Kitty met the boys and Poppy as arranged. Their demeanour told her that Dr Parkin had imparted the news. Patrick was idly playing with a broken pen nib and looking despondent. John was pacing, bright eyed around the room. Poppy seemed intrigued by a broken finger nail.

"Patrick, this could be the ideal opportunity to get to know your uncle as you both recover fully," Kitty started brightly.

"I spoke to him this morning and he talked about my father and what they got up to. It was nice to hear about my father, as I didn't know him that well as he was always travelling with mother. Perhaps it will be alright."

"We have got a plan of sorts," added John. "Patrick is going to write to me once a week or so and if he mentions Bear here —" he indicated their mountainous friend, "—I will know he is in trouble."

In her imagination Kitty saw an indignant John striding into Dr Parkin's office and demanding a rescue party being set up immediately. However, as Dr Parkin and Mrs Titherington were not completely sanguine about the decision, Kitty thought that she could leave it to them to come up with a plan. Although she might sow a seed of an idea before she left. Where was Mr Gregory?

It was shortly after a light luncheon that Patrick and his

guardian were waved off. The boys made jokes and, on the surface, all was fine, with tentative plans in place for a summer visit to John's home. Well, that was obvious, despite a complete lack of real facts she believed that a clergyman sworn to protect his flock could murder his nephew. Never had she felt so powerless.

BACK ON THE ROAD

Travel, especially along this same road, had lost its gilt. Gone was the pleasure of seeing new buildings, observing strangers at work and the smell of new towns. She was certain that she had seen that milkmaid at least three times before.

Poppy was nodding in time to the sway of the carriage. Kitty had to admit to herself that part of the problem with this journey was that she had become used to the comfort and attention a private carriage gave you when compared to the common stage.

Oh my, she was becoming spoilt and entitled. Though looking at Poppy's hands properly for the first time she noted that they were no longer engrained with dirt but were still rough and red from hard work with nails kept short through biting. Her clothes were hand-me-downs and her hair though now brushed, was scraped back with a cap to disguise its condition. Bathing was something that Poppy was still dubious about and washing her hair seemed a complete waste of time. But never had Poppy complained.

A little voice in Kitty's head told her that Poppy's

upbringing had conditioned her to not expecting anything better than she got. While Kitty had been brought up to respect, to be kind and expect kindness in return. Above all, she had received love, nurture and hope. She was indeed spoilt and the only future she was fit for was as wife of a gentleman.

As a governess she would be neither fish nor fowl – servant not family. As a companion she would be the charity case or the unpaid skivvy, depending on the caprice of her employer. Yes indeed, Miss Kitty Lucas was indulging in a satisfying wallow of self-pity.

But above all she did not just want to be someone's wife. It was not that she didn't want to be married but there had to be more, there *was* more. As one of her father's parishioners, Mrs Callow, had remarked, Kitty was too educated to be a good wife. She would change, she would take hold of her destiny. She would set the rules. As she nodded off herself, the little voice whispered to her; Set new rules, just don't break the ones which protect you.

The journey fell into a routine of its own. Tolls were opened and the coach lumbered through disgorging its passengers at one favoured hostelry after another. Some souls only travelled for one or two stages clutching their bandboxes, bundles and baskets. Others required possessions tossed down to them from the roof resulting in curses and threats from their owners.

While theirs was not the newest or best-appointed conveyance on the road but neither was it the most patronised, which meant that they were not crammed in on top of each other. Kitty compared it to her first such trip, which seemed full of interesting characters and promise. Now she barely looked at her fellow passengers; her thoughts concentrating on Patrick and with increasing vehemence on Mr Gregory. Where *was* he? What was he doing?

The steady rumble of the wheels slowed indicating an

approach to a scheduled stop. Poppy still slept but Kitty was uncomfortable; her shoulders stiff, her mouth dry and her head starting to ache dully. Rousing Poppy, she motioned for them to disembark and they were handed out of the carriage by a pleasant-looking man in a brown moleskin jacket and trousers. Turning to thank him she saw him catch a small trunk from the roof before marching off to be met by two small children and their parents. The reunion was full of hugs and laughter as the girls dived into the newcomer's pockets retrieving ribbons and lace as they all walked down the street. Kitty had never felt so alone in her whole life.

"Miss?" Kitty turned and moved out of Poppy's way.

"I'm just making a visit to the barn." And off she scuttled to make her ablutions.

"I will wait by the horse block," she called after her. She spied the large piece of granite substantial enough for a large gentleman to mount any steed in the realm.

As usual baskets of apples, trays of pies as well as cider, beer and milk were being peddled. Having purchased two wrinkled but perfectly good apples and a couple of cold bread buns. She was securing these in her reticule while sitting on the steps of the horse block, when a hand passed her a glass of milk.

Her position and the brim of her bonnet stopped her from glimpsing the face but she recognised the hand. Taking the milk in silence she inspected it closely before taking a sip. It was fresh, rich and creamy and just what she needed. Damn him! He leant on the block proper and sipped from a metal tankard. She did not look at the gleaming boots or perfectly fitted trousers. She certainly did not look at his face. She would not be the first to speak.

"I am surprised, Miss Lucas."

"Really, sir? Why is that?"

"I would have thought that one of the first things a governess taught was good manners."

Flushing, she replied, "Thank you sir, most refreshing."

"And second would have been honesty."

Now she was confused and before she could stop herself, altered position to look at him directly, "Sir?"

"That poor Mrs Wellings. Left without a word or a penny in recompense and in the middle of the night. She was all for sending for the magistrate when we intervened."

Kitty was mortified, she had indeed forgotten all about the Duke's Head. She had not given a moment's thought to the fact that she still had all her belongings, that Poppy must have packed and left in secret and in the middle of the night. Never returning to the Duke's Head was now a priority! Kitty knew her flush had deepened.

"Luckily, we explained about the boy's relapse after your day out and sympathised about finding well-mannered servants, then paid her for her inconvenience."

Kitty said nothing. The calm and pleasant tone he used barely hid his annoyance. They both looked at the courtyard scene before them. The coach was starting to board its passengers and Poppy was walking opened mouthed towards her.

"Thunder n' Turf Miss Lucas you could have all been …" his lips clamped shut as she saw an array of emotions play across his face.

Kitty stood, handed him her glass and with legions of female ancestors behind her said, "Thank you for the refreshment sir, but we must continue with our journey. So nice to meet old acquaintances when travelling."

Her curtsey was perfect, her manner pleasant and calm masking the shame and embarrassment within. With a slight and wry smile, he returned her salute and watched her walk away. Kitty caught Poppy's elbow and steered her towards the coach, hissing under her breath, "Not now."

Their delay in re-boarding meant they were committed to

the middle of the bench, which was a blessing as even if tempted no more than a glimpse of the yard was possible courtesy of a large basket containing daffodils. Once settled, Kitty busied herself with sharing out their fare and eating. Not a word passed between them until the next inn.

Dignity and pride carried Kitty to her aunt's house. If she had thought Epsom was bustling, it was nothing compared to London. If it hadn't been for the coach driver, who saw at once how green they were and found a reputable driver to take them to their final destination, the Lord knows what would have happened to them.

Surprisingly, her aunt had been expecting them and everything was accomplished with ease, including the installation of Poppy as lady's maid. She had been hustled upstairs and given supper in bed.

When she woke, curtains were being twitched aside and a smiling Poppy was urging her to sit and partake of her hot chocolate. Kitty's head felt like wool, but she noticed that Poppy was wearing a neat and prim flowered dress with a high neck and long sleeves, along with a starched apron and hair neatly scraped back under a pristine cap.

"You look very smart, Poppy."

"Thank you, miss. Miss Watkins has set me up good and proper."

"And who is Miss Watkins?"

"Ooh she be your aunt's maid. She is set on training me up like."

"Do you think you'll be happy here?"

"Yes miss. Miss Watkins insisted she write to father and told him where I were and that I'd send him some wages. I will get wages, won't I?"

"Yes, Poppy I will pay you from my allowance each month and you will get board and lodging from my aunt and it looks like training from Miss Watkins."

Sipping at her chocolate, she asked gently: "Poppy can you not read and write?"

"Oh, I can read alright miss but my hand is dreadful. Parson's wife always said it was the worst in the class 'cos I would want to use my left hand."

She busied herself around the room and Kitty watched as she laid out clothes. Every now and then she would stop and check something in her apron pocket and add something else to the selection.

"Am I going out?"

"Yes miss. We're going shopping. Ah, I should have said first. Your aunt will be ready to leave at eleven."

Kitty had always dressed herself and this was probably just as well as Poppy, though eager, was more of a hindrance, so Kitty sent her away in search of something which would do for breakfast. By the time she returned with a plate of bread, ham, cheese and honey Kitty was clothed appropriately with her hair simply dressed in a clear and clean mirror.

Kitty placed the tray on the small side table by the window and then looked at the room. It was clean and light and not at all like the dark panelled rooms or distempered walls she was used to. The grate was simple but the floorboards gleamed and the rugs were thick and soft. The furniture was inlayed with lighter wood and flowers stood on a simple mantelpiece. This was a beautiful room.

As Kitty came downstairs her aunt appeared from a drawing room wearing a staggering plumed hat, tassled cane and sporting a patch on her cheek. Her aunt liked to shop in style. Kitty made her good morning.

"Very prettily done my dear. But, as I thought, you do look too provincial. That we will rectify. What is your girl called?"

"Oh, Poppy, ma'am."

"Aunt will do, but Poppy will not."

"Girl, what is your name?"

A small voice from behind her piped up, "Poppy Foster, ma'am."

"Very well, Watkins and Foster can visit the haberdasher's alone. I think we will need some time." As she spoke she took Kitty's hand turned her this way and that.

Kitty offered her hand as they went down the final sweep to the entrance hall.

"I am not infirm, child. But I will humour you on this occasion."

She leant heavily on Kitty but kept her back straight and her head high. Servants appeared from different directions, opening doors to the street and the carriage. Kitty barely had time to see hawkers with flowers, elegant men on horseback and delivery carts with milk and coal before they were off.

"Never gawk, child," commented her aunt as she looked through the window. Watkins was sitting primly at the edge of the seat and Kitty smiled to see Poppy adjust her posture to emulate her mentor.

When the two maids were set down, her aunt turned to her.

"There are several matters we need to discuss but not here and now. However, something I must make clear. I want a companion because the family say I must have one. I do not want some aged twittering old maid but neither do I want some gadfly. I am not senile and I enjoy the Season. I want someone to enjoy it with. Are we clear?"

"Yes, aunt."

Kitty's only experience of a companion was Miss Hughes, who was very involved in good works and picked up after old Mrs Ferguson, played cards badly and was regularly teased by the rest of the household. This version of the role sounded more appealing.

Aunt Charlotte was her father's sister and had been married briefly. Her husband, Mr Elliot, came with a good fortune and had the good manners to die before it was hardly touched. With no offspring to consider her aunt had then indulged herself in good company and the finer things in life.

Kitty was of the firm opinion that her aunt did not need a companion at all. However, no one with a fortune finds themselves bereft of family. Aunt Charlotte benefitted from two brothers, Kitty's father and her Uncle Henry. As mild-mannered as her father, Henry had married an ambitious lady who had then produced four sons. And it was this Aunt Constance who wanted to assure herself that Charlotte was not squandering her sons' futures. Hence the companion.

When the carriage stopped a second time her aunt fairly leapt from it and Kitty hurried after her into a milliner's. Her aunt was obviously well-known in this establishment, as a foppish man dressed in black hurried over wringing his hands and greeting her in obsequious tones.

If Kitty had been a doll she may have relished the next few hours. But she was not. True, she did love the feel of the feathers and lace, the fresh muslin and smooth percale. But the difference between the three shades of yellow were lost on her as was the discussion over the quality and quantity of ribbon which was appropriate this season.

Her aunt was in her element and bustled Kitty from shop to shop. Kitty became increasingly aware of the number of day dresses, gowns, coats, hats and bonnets that were being totted up. True, her aunt did add an enormous cornette to the list before discarding it for a more fashionable purple turban. As she gave her opinion on the creation, Kitty noticed a growing flush on her aunt's face and neck.

"Aunt would it be possible to have a break, I feel a little light-headed?"

"Girls today, Monsieur Phillipe, have no stamina," said her aunt to the proprietor of the milliners. Then, leaning heavily on Kitty's arm, made her way to the door where the carriage waited patiently.

# RESETTLED

**T**en days since their arrival Kitty was sitting in bed, propped up by clean lace-edged linen pillows, sipping chocolate while nibbling on bread and honey. Her aunt did not hold with breakfast and was rarely seen before noon, so mornings were Kitty's own. Today she had a letter and its contents had robbed her of her appetite.

*Dear Miss Lucas*

*Thank you for sending me your new address. Dr Parkin says that means that I can write to you.*

*I received my second letter from Patrick, and his uncle wants to take him to Italy in September so he won't be coming back here until after Christmas. What will you do? Dr Parkin says I have to stay here but you have got to do something.*

*Mr Gregory arrived the day you left. He was in a bit of a snit.*

*Kindest regards*

Then in another hand, older and neater:

*Patrick's bills were paid by Mssrs Hinch, Forth and Worthy in Lincoln's Inn. I am enclosing a letter of introduction.*

A short note, but to be expected and it answered her question about Mr Gregory finding her on the road. It saddened her that John had not mentioned Poppy but, most importantly, she was now worried to death about Patrick's future.

Absentmindedly, she finished her breakfast while formulating a plan. After pulling the bell for Poppy, she sent a note to her aunt begging the use of the carriage this morning before sitting at her writing desk and beginning her task.

Two hours later, dressed in the most elegant of morning dresses, topped by a very expensive but conservative bonnet she was seated in a cab accompanied by her equally appropriately dressed but stern-looking lady's maid. In the ten days they had been in London, Poppy had been schooled by her aunt's maid and had absorbed the old retainer's attitude to what was and was not suitable. Privately, Kitty wondered how much would take long-term but she kept her thoughts and her smiles to herself.

Lincoln's Inn, like the rest of the city, was bustling. Clerks carried briefs wrapped in ribbons, messengers scurried between chambers, courts and the whole plethora of officialdom. Plaintiffs and defendants wandered, some with aplomb others in trepidation, while on the side lines hawkers of delights (legal and illegal) perched and in the shadows lurked cutpurses and runners each wary of the other.

Kitty found the scene fascinating and watched from the carriage for a while before alighting. This was not a place for a lady alone with her maid and as she stepped down after her, Kitty heard Poppy take in a deep breath. Something she did every time she had to venture out of the streets of the *bon monde*. Robert, the footman led the way.

The offices of Hinch, Forth and Worthy were old and well cared for; the epitome of respectability. If they were surprised to see her they did not so much as betray it with a look but escorted her to an office redolent with wax, snuff and leather.

What she was not prepared for was the pair of elegant crossed legs belonging to the reclining figure of Mr Gregory. He was flicking open a Limoges snuff box as she entered and though he paused briefly and acknowledged her entry with a slight incline of the head, he continued with the manoeuvre before standing and offering her his chair with an exaggerated flourish.

Any butterflies that might have been lurking flew away in fear as her jaw clenched and she took the proffered seat with a slight nod in his direction.

"We seem…" she began. He raised his finger almost imperceptibly and she halted. The door shut behind the clerk, he lowered his hand and turned to face her. She began again, "Mr Gregory…" Only to be stopped by the door opening and an older gentleman entering dressed in subdued clothing befitting his profession: white stockings, black buckled shoes and long fitted jacket covering sombre breeches.

As she raised her eyes to his pristine stock and pleasant red-cheeked face he felt like a family friend and eminently trustworthy. She returned his smile and felt Mr Gregory walk behind her resting one hand lightly on her shoulder. A warning or a something more proprietary? Irritatingly, it stopped her long enough for him to get the first words of greeting in, which she surmised was his intention all along as his hand was then removed. She seethed in silence, which again was probably what he intended.

"Thank you for seeing us, Mr Hinch, as I explained to your clerk we are in urgent need of your advice concerning one of your clients."

Mr Hinch walked to the opposite side of the desk and lowered himself down with the care used by those susceptible to a gouty foot. Following him came a different clerk with two files which he placed before the legal gentleman and then stood to one side. Kitty thought that if he could have blended in completely with the wainscoting he would have felt much more comfortable.

"An unusual request, sir, and you mentioned that it was concerning the estate of the late Mr and Mrs Templeton. But I do not see how I can help you."

"I believe you are one of the trustees for their son, Patrick?"

"Yes, that is so, but …"

"Then I feel that I must take you into our confidence. But first I think that you would be justified in seeing our credentials. Sister?"

The warning hand was back on the shoulder, stifling the questions she had on her lips. Opening her reticule Kitty passed the letter of introduction to her *darling* brother. How on Earth had he… enlightenment came; she donned her most winning smile though her eyes flashed with thoughts of just what she was going to say to Poppy, never mind Mr Gregory. Sister indeed! But then she had the letter of introduction and he did not.

Mr Hinch opened the letter nodding as he did so.

"Dr Parkin is a most excellent educationalist. I found his knowledge on the fauna of the New Forest quite enlightening, or was it Dartmoor?"

Kitty smiled, "I am sure he is most well informed on both sir, though his current enthusiasm seems to lie with rhododendron."

Mr Hinch relaxed. He was testing us surmised Kitty. She smiled hopefully in a manner that authors would describing as winning rather than smirking.

"As you are probably aware, Patrick was recently the victim of an abduction. The perpetrators are still at large and we are concerned that Patrick is still in danger. I believe that the Last Will and Testament of his parents may hold some clue as to motive."

"But surely the proper authorities …"

"Are more interested in solving crimes rather than preventing them."

Kitty intervened, "Surely the document has been published so there can be no conflict in interest in showing it to us and as my brother said that is not the main reason for our visit."

"Indeed, we believe the document can give us some information but then we need your advice as a legal man on how to proceed to protect Patrick."

Mr Hinch pondered with him hands prayer-like to his lips. "It is unusual but not illegal." With that he nodded towards his clerk, who leapt forward undoing one of the folders and placing the document on the table before Kitty, where both she and Mr Gregory could read it. The legalese was tortuous but she had read worse in her father's library of clerical pronouncements.

The estate was held in trust until Patrick was twenty-one with Dr Parkin, Mr Hinch and his uncle as trustees. There were bequests to people Kitty had never heard of but if Patrick died before reaching his majority the whole of the estate went to Geraint Templeton-Hughes and his descendants. A fairly typical document of its kind with major life changes such as marriage to be approved by his trustees. But as young as Patrick was this was not relevant.

"Should his uncle predecease him who would become the trustee?"

"Oh, that would be Claude Templeton-Hughes, his son."

Mr Gregory asked other questions about lands in Hanover and ownership of a boat held at Dover as well as any unhappy creditors. At a suitable pause in the conversation she asked, "May I ask the profession of Mr Claude Templeton-Hughes?"

"He follows that of his father, madam, he is a minister of the church."

"You have been most helpful Mr Hinch, so to bring us back to the reason for our visit, Patrick and his guardian are planning to visit Italy after the summer. I would like your support, along with Dr Parkin, in strongly suggesting a bodyguard accompany them. I have contacted the Runners and they have proposed one of their own as a suitable man."

"Assuming that the culprits are not brought to justice."

"Quite so."

"Then I think your plan a good one, Mr Lucas."

With that the pleasantries were concluded and Mr and Miss Lucas left the premises accompanied by a contrite Poppy. No words were spoken on the walk back to her carriage. He handed Kitty in, bowed and simply walked away.

As the carriage moved off, Kitty turned to Poppy: "I think you have some explaining to do."

Through the snufflings, pleas and promises, Kitty pieced together the story. Poppy had been charged by Mr Clark, Pip's erstwhile Runner, to keep him informed of any correspondence and resulting actions on Kitty's part. He had stressed in quite stark terms, what would happen to Poppy if anything happened to her mistress. Kitty seethed. She forgave Poppy immediately but fumed that the man could have frightened a mere child who had known little of stability and

care in her short life by threatening her with the horrors of a
London bereft of reference, roof or protector. However, she
did now know of a way of contacting Mr Gregory should the
need arise or of sending him of on a false trail should she
need to.

Their return to Hanover Square coincided with the serving of luncheon. Having no time to change, Kitty charged Poppy with her outer clothing before joining her aunt. Although she raised an eyebrow at her attire no comment was made.

"I am at home this afternoon Ki…. Mmm, I think we will return to Katherine, you are a woman, not a child. And should Lady Armstrong decide to bring her nasty little grandson with her, I trust you can keep his spoiled little fingers away from my Spode."

"Certainly aunt. Do we have any spillikins I could distract him with?"

"I doubt it."

"I will see what I can contrive. Are you expecting many visitors?"

"Quite a few I fancy will want to look you over and see how far in my dotage I am. Wear the sprig muslin, child. Garstang, is that ground rice mould? Excellent."

Garstang always waited on luncheon and as he helped Kitty

to some of the pudding he whispered that he would send some tapers up to her from the kitchen. She smiled her thanks.

Sated, her aunt went to answer her correspondence leaving Kitty alone sitting on the window seat watching the street scene below her. The garden in the centre of the square was being planted out with summer plants, nursemaids were dragging or being dragged along the pavement, but there was little movement else. The main visiting times would be in around two hours when carriages would make their sedate way through the streets as the most connected and influential in society started their day. They were a beautiful sight and sitting at the periphery Kitty had the best seat in the house.

A cough brought her back to the room, Garstang stood with a handful of spills.

"Thank you, Mr Garstang."

"My pleasure Miss Katherine. I took the liberty of bringing your watercolours. Shall I send Foster to you?"

"No need, I think."

He bowed but not before laying a large napkin over the back of the chair. Smiling, she spent some time colouring the ends of the sticks and sticking them in the vases on the mantelpiece to dry. A real task that pleased her with its completion and simplicity. Also, with her hands occupied it allowed her mind to come up with a plan. Smiling she went to change for the afternoon's social whirl.

Poppy was still cowed and Kitty decided to let her suffer a little more and chose not to speak to her apart from making her preferences for sashes clear. Poppy sniffed but it left Kitty unmoved, a contrite unquestioning Poppy was what she needed for her plan to work.

Aunt Charlotte's hosting was well regarded and she had many friends who filled both drawing rooms. The spills were needed as a number of the ladies brought a grandchild and a fairly raucous game was overseen by Kitty in the library. With a combination of charades, milk, cake and storytelling she kept her charges out of the way until time to return them angel-like to their doting grandmamas who left with them as with a badge of honour.

Only three elderly ladies were left in the drawing room with her aunt by now. With a nod to Garstang, he replaced the teacups with glasses of madeira. Kitty sat in the window seat again and was also offered a glass. She sipped it. It was sweet but completely unlike the Elder wine she had helped make each year at home.

She tuned into the conversations going on around her until she settled on one voice which pricked Kitty's attention.

"Of course, I knew her, she married the same year as you dear Charlotte. Four daughters and one son, never have I seen William so happy. Though daughters are well enough a man always wants a boy. Now don't tut at me Maria, you know it's the truth as well as I."

"I still thought it was heartless to flaunt her grandson when she must have known poor Mrs Bottomley would be here."

"Because Clara Bottomley and Harriet Blair have been friends for ever."

"Dearest, you must have heard. Sir Thomas read it from the newspaper this very morning."

"William's youngest grandson – only fourteen you know. Yes, his poor body was washed up at Folkestone."

"Well yes, he was unhappy at school, but running away is never the way. Such a waste, and the scandal…"

"Really Charlotte. Harriet's pearls, the ones William gave her when John was born. You need to pay attention dear, really."

"They are saying he took them."

"Geraint."

"Her grandson – really Charlotte do keep up."

Kitty found herself back at The Towers and the thwarted

Claudius. Was it a coincidence? Was this the fate that had awaited him? What had happened to the curious curate Mr Bostock? She realised that she hadn't given him a thought since she had left The Towers.

The general conversation moved to others deaths and illnesses of friends until the little French clock sang the hour. Gasps of horror and claims about the the lack of time to plan the evening's activities accompanied the collection of reticules, cloaks and pelisses before the swishing of skirts and closing of doors welcomed in calm and quiet.

"Aunt, may I borrow a newspaper?"

"Yes dear, of course, the Times will be in the library. You did very well this afternoon. I think we deserve a treat. Clara was talking about a new play at the Theatre Royal. I would not take you if Kean was playing after his treatment of Mrs Porter, most unworthy of him. But Clara says that it is quite spectacular."

The newspaper was indeed in the library but the details were no more than she had gleaned from that afternoon's conversation. Up until this morning she had no way of contacting Mr Gregory. She needed information but maybe she could do this without him. She went in search of the butler.

"Mr Garstang, how do I find out about names and departures of ships?"

If he was surprised he showed it not at all. After a moment's reflection he informed her that Lloyd's List would be the very thing and furthermore he would obtain her a copy.

There was one more thing she needed to check. Back in her aunt's library she quickly found a copy of the Clerical Guide. Turning the pages, she realised that this was arranged by county and was published in 1817. Where could she find the most recent information? Looking again she found an address, 62, St Paul's Churchyard, London.

Returning to her room she copied the address into her silver *aide memoir*, she traced the intricate carving of lilies and daisies. Her father had given it to her last Christmas. It had been her mother's *carnet de bal*, and the first bone page still held the pencilled name of her father in her mother's childlike writing.

Although Kitty had no idea what you wore to the theatre, Poppy had been well prepared by Miss Watkins. This was confirmed when Kitty realised that she was wearing a similar palette to her aunt, but more subdued. The lilac suited Kitty and the purple matched the turban though now it was adorned with more feathers and jewels which were certainly not paste. Kitty's personal jewels were restricted to a single string of pearls, which she now wore and which passed the critical glance of her aunt.

The theatre was incredible. Her aunt approved the new portico which welcomed them and Kitty was astounded to see (and smell) the gas lighting. But most of all it was the number of people which she found most affecting and troubling, she was glad when they were led to a box.

She had been to plays before as a special treat but here the actors were less exaggerated in their movements and the audience listened instead of talked. The lighting was used to heighten the atmosphere as the mood darkened, and hell was depicted by real rain on stage as the hero fled onto the blasted heath. She was entranced.

"You are enjoying it, my dear?"

"It is truly wonderful, aunt, thank you."

"No, my dear, it is amusing or cleverly produced, never wonderful."

"But …"

"Now move your chair slightly as this is when friends will visit."

Kitty stood and moved to the rear of the box as her aunt's contemporaries arrived to discuss other theatregoers and their dresses. They were then joined by their spouses and escorts who smelled as if they had indulged in liquid refreshment as well as a chance to stretch their legs. She moved into a corner but keeping an eye on her aunt for cues. She was not introduced as her aunt held court so was surprised when she heard herself addressed:

"Are you enjoying the performance, Miss Lucas?"

She turned to look at the bluest eyes she had ever seen. As before, they were laughing.

"Yes, thank you, Mr … Gregory."

"Edward dear, you are here," cried her aunt. She beckoned him over and, bowing, he left her side and bowed low over her aunt's hand brushing her glove with his lips.

"Clara, you've met by godson, Edward? Of course, oh they are dimming the lights."

As the crowd thinned to retake their seats, her aunt patted the chair next to her and Edward sat in it. Kitty moved to take the chair at the back of the box. Suddenly her aunt turned around,

"Where are you? Come on, take your seat, dear."

She patted the seat on the other side of her, finished her madeira which had magically appeared in her hand and promptly fell asleep. Kitty was alarmed.

"It is her custom, Miss Lucas. But she will need you to fill in the plot for her on the way home."

"You did not say that you were acquainted with my aunt."

"No, I didn't."

He gently took the glass from the old lady's hand. Any further conversation was curtailed by the complete dimming of the house lights.

Despite her frustrations, the story soon had Kitty in its thrall and she almost cried out when real flames depicting hell appeared in the final scene. The rapturous applause wakened her aunt and as the actors were taking their bows.

Mr Gregory stood. "I will see to the carriage. Wait here until the crush eases."

As soon as the final bow was taken the audience seemed to rise *en masse* and make its way to the exits. The noise was deafening and Kitty was grateful once more that she was in a box. As she looked around her she realised that there were more people in this one theatre than in her entire home village.

She wanted to talk to Mr Gregory but this was impossible as she guided Aunt Charlotte to their carriage.

"Good night ladies, I shall call on you properly tomorrow." And he was gone.

Again.

The next morning her customary hot chocolate was delivered with a copy of Lloyd's List sitting neatly folded still warm from its ironing. Poppy had recovered her usual demeanour and busied herself with organising the tweeny who had brought the water.

Slipping on her robe Kitty sat at a small table spreading the paper before her and sipping her drink.

Lloyd's List was only published twice a week and Mr Garstang had thoughtfully provided her with the last four editions. The problem was that until she saw it, she didn't really know what she was looking for.

The information on stocks did not interest her but the details of boats sunk, run aground or lost did. Mr Garstang had been quite right, this is just what she needed. She found herself fascinated by reports of icebergs, of the Morgiana Sloop of War detaining the Prince of Brazil (a ship she supposed rather than a royal personage) on suspicion of slave trading off the coast of Africa and of pirates in the Mediterranean. Who knew such a paper would be full of wonders and adventure.

She became conscious of Poppy sighing deeply. Her bed

was made and her clothes laid out. Finishing her now cooled chocolate, she washed and dressed. Glimpsing the time on bedroom clock, she told Poppy to fetch her coat as she had something to collect. Giving Poppy no time to report, even if she had wanted to, she placed her bonnet and while she added gloves, shawl and parasol to her ensemble in front of the hall mirror, she asked Mr Garstang to acquire a hackney carriage.

Clean but aged, the carriage made its ponderous way to St Paul's Churchyard.

Kitty had high hopes of St Paul's. Her father always spoke of it as an emblem of hope so she was somewhat underwhelmed by the dreary area she found herself in. The weak sun had not made it through the cloud and like everywhere else humanity abounded but somehow while it was certainly very large, she was not moved by it.

Entering the body of the building was not illuminating either, it was dark and damp and she would have been ashamed to have been responsible for the state of the brasses and wood she saw. However, there did seem to be building or restoration work underway so perhaps cleanliness was not possible.

Beckoning Poppy close, they left and having acquired a couple of choristers as guides for a promise of a few coppers, they found themselves on St Paul's Churchyard and in a very few minutes were at the offices of the Clerical Guide.

Kitty found herself on firmer ground here than at the lawyer's offices. Although the next edition of the guide itself was not due to be published for two years, the business of collating and updating the positions was bobbing along with a Mr George Clarence at its helm. He was a young man with a slight stoop from hunkering over books in a not-particularly well-lit office with natural light limited to a single grimy window. He kept sneaking peeks at the two female creatures who had invaded his world. Never quite making eye contact, he was a definite mine of information.

However, having checked the counties of Somerset, Wiltshire, Berkshire and Gloucestershire she had found only one Templeton-Hughes and no Mr Bostock. Letting a long sigh of exasperation escape her, Mr Clarence spoke.

"Was it a particular gentleman you were looking for?"

She turned and, with one look at her face, he went scuttling towards a set of tall thin drawers.

"We do have an alphabetical list as well as a geographical one, you see…"

He ground to halt and Kitty admonished herself for not being more precise in her request.

Smiling sweetly, she requested the name Templeton-Hughes. Geraint she had already found in the county lists, but she wanted to determine if he had a son in holy orders. She was not sure whether she was disappointed to find Claude had his own listing. He had a parish in Kent. Returning to county listings they found him in the small parish of Graine.

"Would you have a list of curates or other officers of the church here?"

"You would need to go to the Parish for that, or maybe the Bishop would know? Was it anyone in particular?"

"A Mr Bostock."

He returned to his lists but the only gentlemen he found had been established in their parishes for some time and Kitty estimated they would be too old for the man she was after. On a whim she recorded the names of the three men the clerk found for her. Having left him some money, 'to treat him to luncheon for his efforts', they left.

Finding a carriage for hire on her own was something Kitty had not thought about. Guessing that the best course was to return to the cathedral, that is what they did. As nature likes balance, or God was on their side, Kitty's hard work was graced by that elusive madame, Lady Fortune. As they were waiting for a party of elderly ladies to extricate themselves from a hackney carriage she caught sight of a man closely resembling Mr Bostock. Grabbing Poppy by the arm, they followed.

He was dressed as were so many of the clergy around her. It might not be him. But there was something in his manner and walk that made her think of Mr Bostock and he had been very much in her thoughts. Shushing Poppy's protests they entered the nave. Keen to keep her prey in her sights they moved down towards the quire. Their quarry skirted the scaffolding and workmen and disappeared behind the quire screen. Unsure of the layout Kitty spied a party being given a tour and heading towards the crypt to view Lord Nelson's tomb. They added themselves to the back of the tour.

With hindsight this was not her most successful plan. True, she now knew that Nelson's black marble sarcophagus was originally made for Cardinal Wolsey and they did have an acceptable reason for their excursion and late return to Hanover Square, but she was none the wiser as to the whereabouts of Mr Bostock or Claude Templeton-Hughes.

The next few days Kitty applied herself to the support of her aunt in her daily rounds having spent the mornings perusing the Lloyd's Lists, which Mr Garstang diligently placed on her morning tray, answering her and her aunt's correspondence. Which is how she knew Mr Gregory was out of town, as he had sent a note of thanks for the theatre and explained that he would be away for a few days but looked forward to taking his godmother for a drive when he returned. Her emotions were mixed on reading this, but frustration best described them. Never mind, she would continue alone.

Afternoons were a varied but constant round of visiting her aunt's acquaintance and chewing over the latest gossip.

Kitty also got to know the household much better and gained an insight into her relative's finances. Keeping a carriage, Kitty knew, was not cheap but for her aunt it was an essential. A cook, two maids and Mr Garstang ran the establishment with the aid of the two lady's maids, her Poppy included, but though her aunt insisted on the best food she was not above remodelling gowns and hats. She set herself one evening excursion a week during the season which saved on the expense of gowns but also meant that she bestowed on events a certain prestige by her patronage – or so she informed Kitty.

About a week after her frustrating trip to the cathedral a letter from her father arrived. Kitty had sent him the obligatory letter announcing her safe arrival but didn't really expect a letter from him by return. His letter was full of the news of births, illnesses, recoveries and deaths. Mrs Walters was getting to grips with the Sunday School since Kitty had left and he had had an afternoon fishing with Mr Walters the day before. She felt a tug of homesickness but her father was quite self-sufficient and perfectly happy reading his books and visiting his flock.

After breakfast she sat in the small library, which was fast becoming her favourite room, and sorted the cards left the previous day and a new set of invitations. She had started to make a careful tally of who had called and if they had had their kindness returned. Her aunt was quite punctilious in this matter but her memory was fading, which had almost led to a blunder a few days ago. As a consequence, Kitty slid into the dual role of companion and secretary.

Having finished with her aunt's affairs she began on the letter to her father, detailing all she could remember of St Paul's, when there came a scraping on the door followed by Mr Garstang.

"Excuse me, miss, but a gentleman has called."

"Aunt Catherine in not receiving today and—" she glanced at the clock, "—certainly not this early."

"I explained that to the gentleman, but as he said he is known to you he said he would like to speak to you."

"Me? Who?"

"A Mr Gregory, miss. He is known to madam, and so I have shown him into the drawing room. Shall I fetch Foster, Miss?"

"Thank you, yes please Mr Garstang."

Confused, she straightened her dress and hair before meeting Poppy on the stairs and confronting Mr Gregory. And just what was this feeling in the pit of her stomach all about?

Standing next to the cold grate – heating unused rooms not being one of her aunt's essentials – was the impossibly handsome Mr Gregory. His hair was curled and styled to look un-styled and, as she opened the door, he was taking a pinch of snuff. He dropped the powder and snapped the pretty Limoges box shut, before making his bow. Kitty returned it and Poppy picked up some sewing in the window. Miss Watkins's training apparently.

White pantaloons, a deep blue tailcoat and exquisite white shirt with a high colour and blue linen at the throat.

"Mr Gregory, please take a seat."

Sitting herself opposite, she found herself intrigued by his tie, "Is that the Mathematical?"

"Of sorts. It is known as the Irish Tie. I was not aware you were an expert on men's fashion, Miss Lucas."

"Nor am I. But listening to fond grandmother's describing their grandchild's attempt at an Osbaldeston or Napoleon has enthused me with naming and scoring each necktie I see."

"I don't doubt it."

He looked a warning at her before glancing at Poppy still intent on the piece of sewing in her hands.

"Do you not recognise Poppy, sir?"

He stood and looked directly at the young girl. Poppy in her turn looked at him full in the face and laughed.

"I see that you have both found your niche. How are you enjoying London?"

"London is what it is, sir. However, shall we dispense with the pleasantries?" she leaned forwards. "Mr Gregory, is Patrick safe?"

"To be equally blunt, no."

"What were you looking for at Mr Hick's office?"

"The same as you, I wanted sight of the full will. I didn't find what I was after. Did you?"

"Yes. I had thought the uncle was the seat of the trouble but now I believe it is his son, Claude."

"How did you find out about Claude?"

"I looked him up in the Clerical Register."

"And there was me running up and down to Oxford and Bath. I found he was in Kent. And you?"

"Graine. It is in Kent."

Mr Gregory gave an admiring smile. "Indeed it is. Once an island, it is marshy, lonely and on the coast with a reputation for nightly nefarious dealings."

"You mean smuggling."

"Yes."

"Then why not say so."

"But…"

"I have waited over a week for you to do the courtesy of telling me…" An epiphany hit her.

"Does Aunt Charlotte know about all this?"

"Some. She knows we met at The Towers and I dropped in on her when I made London and mentioned that I had passed you on the road and when she should expect you. She was quite curt actually, so I made sure Clarky secured you a decent conveyance from the stage."

"I see." Silence followed for a few moments until, "So am I on the right track?"

"I think so. Claude is well-known for gambling and left

debts behind him in Bath and Oxford which his father bought off. His uncle, Patrick's father, purchased a living for him. I think both brothers thought that an out of the way place in Kent would be ideal, but you can gamble most places. While Geraint loves horseflesh he does not gamble, never has in fact, but I think young Claude must have got a taste for it at an early age. Patrick's father married late and Claude thought of his uncle's not insignificant wealth as his by right."

"If something should happen to Patrick … but why wait – what if something should happen to both his father and his cousin."

Mr Gregory leaned forward with excitement. "Especially now they have said they are travelling abroad?"

"Persephone."

…And then leaned back. "I beg your pardon?"

"Persephone. We thought it was a horse. What if it was a boat?"

"A boat? Why a boat?"

"Yes. When I heard about poor William Blair or was it Bottomley. Anyway, one of them, had been drowned at sea having stolen his grandmother's pearls, I started perusing Lloyd's List for clues."

"You do seem to have a penchant for lists, Miss Lucas. But what is this about pearls?"

Ignoring him she continued, warming to her theme: "Do you not see any parallels? What if Mr Bostock and Claude Hughes-Templeton were in it together."

"Templeton-Hughes."

"Quite. Well Graine is by the sea, maybe he had a boat called Persephone. Maybe they knew each other from Oxford was it or somewhere else. What if he meant for Patrick to be on the same boat as Geraint?"

"There are a lot of maybes and what ifs. Graine is a long way from Bath and there are quicker routes to take to find boats. Also, we have no idea where Mr Bostock went after the incident at Easter."

"He is in London."

Mr Gregory was surprised a second time. "I beg your pardon?"

"He is in London we saw him last week."

"Where?"

"At St Paul's."

"The cathedral?"

"Yes, of course!"

"I think Graine may be a red herring. Where was the boy found?"

"Which boy? William? Folkestone."

"Have you found a Persephone in the lists?"

"No, though to be honest I have been looking for the name Bostock and I only just made the connection."

"I think we have to call it a possibility of a connection. Have you got a copy of the List? Never mind, it will be out of date. I need to go to the offices themselves."

"We."

"I beg your pardon?" he asked, frowning.

"We. It was my idea and I have been pursuing it. I want to go too."

"Don't sound petulant."

"Petulant?"

"Yes."

"Well."

A stifled giggling came from the window seat and they both glared at a now innocent-looking Poppy intent on unpicking a very tricky hem. Sobered, Mr Gregory continued in a gentler tone:

"I will go to the offices alone but I promise to report back this afternoon. I told my godmother I would take her for a drive in the park and she will want to go with her companion I'm sure."

He stood to take his leave but she stopped him.

"Mr Gregory, why are you involved in all of this?"

"Did I not mention it?"

She looked at him earnestly and waited it out.

"Miss Lucas. I have from time to time been asked to solve little problems for … well, let us say, illustrious personages."

"That sounds a little sordid, Mr Gregory."

"I agree, but I don't have the skill or aptitude for solving the problems I think you have in mind. And I think your aunt would be scandalised to know that your mind bent that way."

"You are changing the subject. Please stop the flummery and answer the question."

"Very well. What the Ton like to call the recent unpleasantness across the Channel and those involved call a war, led to much upheaval or people, fortune and ideas."

Kitty nodded but did not want to stop the now loquacious Mr Gregory.

"There are always changes in society but developments in transport and the changing nature of manufacture is starting to throw people together more than in previous years. With those changes come ideas and some are dangerous."

"Most are based on inequality and fairness."

"Adam Smith did not see his book as …. but this is not the time for such a debate. Certain people believe that if the ruling class (in which we are both enrolled) does not keep a clean stable…"

"Then Hercules will appear?"

"Please Miss Lucas, flippancy does not suit you. It would only take a scandal to give fuel to a movement to change the old order for a new one. The ruling class must police itself if Britain is not to go the way of the Continent."

"But these are old ideas flouted during the French revolution, surely…"

"We are in the midst of a new revolution, Miss Lucas. One which society can assimilate as long as the new holders of wealth and power want to become members. If certain members of the Ton act as if they were above law and order, there will be complete upheaval."

"Are you saying you police the Ton?"

"Nothing so vulgar. I am usually asked to intervene in issues which would reflect badly on the Crown or…"

"But what has this to do with Patrick?"

"His parents were great favourites at court here and in Hanover."

"But this has nothing to do with…"

"If you cannot see that a scandal involving the son of a favourite of the old king could not be used by enemies of this country, then I am afraid you are naïve."

"I think you exaggerate."

"Have you read the newssheets today, Miss Lucas? No, you are not their audience. They talk of excess, corruption and uncertainty and are stoked by underemployment and lack of food."

He had become quite animated then visibly checked himself and stepped towards the window. He stood with his hands clasped behind his back, staring out. Both girls stared open-mouthed at this new version of Mr Gregory. Poppy looked a question at Kitty who was trying to marry the different facets of the man.

Suddenly he turned to face Kitty. Bowed in silence and left before she could even stand to take her leave.

# HOW TO ACT

Never one to take a great deal of interest in her clothes, that afternoon Kitty was onto her third outfit before she declared herself satisfied.

Aunt Charlotte had also taken a little extra care with her equipage that afternoon too. Going for a drive in the park was a matter of being seen, and even a provincial greenhorn like Kitty knew that.

True to his word a barouche appeared with the top down. The coats of matching chestnut horses shone as did the dark blue body of the coach. A liveried driver completed the elegance. The inside was upholstered in blue brocade and was wonderfully comfortable. The two ladies sat together facing forward with Mr Gregory with his back to the driver. He offered them a cover for their knees and managed to do this by steering clear of the obsequious, and instead sounding sincerely solicitous.

The horses were well-schooled and navigated the busy streets without incident until they found themselves in Hyde Park. Kitty had ventured out once with Poppy along the fenced off walkway beside Rotten Row, but this was the first time she had driven along it. Sedate driving was the rule and even that was difficult as they kept being hailed by acquaintances on horseback or in an array of high-wheeled phaetons, curricles and chaises.

After a second successful circuit they soon found themselves back at home. His godmother insisted he come in for some refreshment and he accepted, sending the carriage home rather than keep his horses standing around.

After a revitalising orgeat, Aunt Charlotte promptly fell asleep. Taking the glass from her opening hand, Kitty put it on the table. The almond cordial was a little too sweet for Kitty and she put her own glass alongside. Mr Gregory had opted for brandy and swirled this in his glass thoughtfully.

Kitty sat and looked at him restraining her now considerable impatience. His attention returned to the room and he smiled at her. He had never smiled at her before and it had a curious effect on her stomach. He was again the urbane member of the Ton. She would take her lead from him, but the encounter had unsettled her and though she did trust him with regard to Patrick, she had come to realise that he was playing a different and longer game than she was.

"There is a ship called the Persephone registered to a man called Cookham. She sails regularly from Dover but is registered in Poole."

"Does this give us anything to act on?" she asked.

"Our working hypothesis is that Claude will try to assassinate his father and cousin. The best plan is to do this on a sea crossing or during their time on the continent. We think we foiled his original attempt to dispose of the boy at sea which we think Mr Bostock was embroiled in."

"I agree. So, what can we do?"

He lifted his brandy to his lips but did not drink before returning it to his lap. "Our options are limited. The original kidnap points to the uncle not the cousin so pursuing that would be counterproductive and the evidence is at best circumstantial."

"Claude wants money but obviously not seriously enough that he cannot wait three months," Kitty said.

"What are you suggesting?"

"Could we make his need for money more urgent?" she said.

"So, he brings his plans forward? But what if he changes them?"

"We may have to talk to the Reverend Hughes-Templeton."

"Templeton-Hughes," he corrected abstractedly.

"But where does Mr Bostock become involved? How do they know each other? We can't just leave Mr Bostock to roam free."

"I agree. But Patrick and his uncle are safe in Langley for the time being. Let us concentrate on the Bostock creature. A link between Claude and him may be a way forward."

Aunt Charlotte awoke suddenly, looked around her, saw Kitty's nearly full glass, downed it and promptly returned to the arms of Morpheus.

"We could start with the cathedral."

"Can you draw a likeness of him?"

"No. One of the reasons I chose companion over governess was my lack of drawing skill."

"A pity."

"It certainly is. Can you sketch him?"

"No. One of the reasons I chose…" he broke off smiling at her again. He really needed to stop doing that. "Then we must set watch."

"I could attempt to sketch some of the interiors for father."

"I thought you couldn't draw."

"They do not have to be any good, no one is going to see them. And if you and Clarky can interview the builders, clerics and coffee shops… I can manage a couple of hours in the morning, in fact I could go for the Eucharist and stay on."

That said, she rose and gently roused her aunt who acted as if she had not been asleep. "Edward, I will be attending your sister's ball. Kindly inform your mother. And thank you for a pleasant afternoon although it has quite done me in. Katherine, ring for Watkins. I will rest before dinner. Edward, there will be cards won't there?"

"I will insist upon it, ma'am."

Bowing low, he departed giving an additional nod to Kitty as he did so.

Although Kitty and Poppy had gone prepared to the cathedral, it was deadly dull. The Eucharist was lovely and made Kitty think lovingly of her father and reminded her that she must finish the letter to him. But for three days they had ambled around the pillars and structures taking each in. They had slotted into guided parties. They had even spent a whole hour sketching the coronet on the top of Nelson's tomb. They had indeed seen clerics galore but not the man they were after. Tomorrow was Sunday, perhaps Kitty could encourage her aunt to attend matins. She looked around the arcade and domes, at the screens, balustrades and gilt grills. Then she saw him. Not Bostock, but Clarky.

Looking like another of the workmen he was leaning on a column but watching a man in the choir. Kitty grabbed Poppy's arm and pulled her close. They could make out a figure laying out music and choristers filing in. It made sense. Bostock had obviously had a way with boys so that they both confided in him and trusted him. But was he a member of the choir himself or a teacher?

The last thing she wanted was to be recognised so leaving Clarky to it, they made their way home. Just as they were about to hail a carriage, Kitty had an idea. Looking around she accosted the first clerically dressed man she saw:

"I am sorry to bother you sir, but I was wondering if you could give me some advice. My mother is very keen for my brother to become a chorister as he has such a sweet voice, but she is concerned that he may not be up to standard. Do you know of any of the choir masters who give private lessons?"

He couldn't give her a name but directed her to the choir school in Cheapside. As she turned away she in turn was accosted by a redoubtable lady who introduced herself as Maria Hackett and wanted Miss Lucas's name to add to a letter she was sending to the Dean about the lamentable education and care received by the boys in the Choir School. After such a breathless and passionate recitation, Kitty felt she had no alternative but to add her name and expressed herself surprised and agreed that her imaginary mother would be best looking elsewhere for musical education. However, news that the choristers would be often found roaming the streets rather than acquiring a more classical education gave her another avenue to explore.

Returning home in better spirits, Kitty decided that this was as good a time as any to finish that letter to her father but as soon as she stepped over the threshold this good intention was forestalled.

"There you are! Child this way, this minute."

Aunt Charlotte was at the head of the stairs, swathed in brocade and satin.

"I have been waiting by the window. I woke this morning with a wonderful idea for the Gregory ball next week."

With that she turned on her heel and returned to the small drawing room with a train of fabric, ladies in lace hats and girls carrying pins in her wake.

Removing her hat as she mounted the stairs she passed these to Poppy while giving her two tasks to complete for her.

The room was full of bolts of cloth and disappointed endeavour. A fire had been lit and the atmosphere was a little thick. But it was her aunt's heightened complexion combined with her heavy breathing with caught Kitty's attention.

"How long have they been at this, Mr Garstang?"

"Since shortly after you left, Miss."

"Mr Garstang could we offer some refreshment to these ladies downstairs? And perhaps Mrs Robinson could provide something fortifying for my aunt?"

Kitty went to the window and opened the sash as Mr Garstang quietly removed the seamstresses. Kitty in turn removed the fabric from her aunt and placed the heavy but beautiful materials on the chaise. She found that Mr Garstang had returned with a glass of sherry.

"Aunt, please, sit for a while. Sip this and explain."

Aunt Charlotte's wonderful idea concerned some fabric she had acquired from a friendly neighbourhood nabob the previous year but hadn't had time to use. The silk lay on a chair and was in the process of being matched with other fabrics.

"But why aunt? Surely there isn't enough time…"

"Nonsense, Bryson is a superb worker and will be well able to create two new creations."

"Two? Why two?"

"Well, we must match. That is the point."

"But aunt…."

Mr Garstang and a maid appeared with a tray and calmly began to set out the repast for two on a small table."

"Aunt, please eat. Now you were going to ensure that I knew the difference between piquet and vingt-et-un before tonight."

Thus distracted, her aunt ate the omelette, took cheese and another glass of sherry.

"I think I have the niceties now, but perhaps we could play a hand to ensure I have it. What exactly did you have in mind for the ball?"

A smile towards Mr Garstang ensured that the table was cleared and a short while after the renowned Mrs Bryson and her team returned.

While Kitty's initial response had been to deny the need for a new dress, she had decided that the wiser course was to follow her aunt's wishes but to try and rein in the wider flights of fancy.

"Beautiful aunt, just like the one Lady Longden had."

"That line is lovely, not many women can carry that off."

"Mrs Bryson, isn't the combination of brocade, lace and feather a little ageing?"

Having pulled in the excess and extravagance, Kitty then had to admire the dressmaker's expertise in combining the fabrics and draping them in such a way that the final effect was obvious. With her aunt satisfied and undraped, she turned to Kitty.

"Now ..."

"Aunt, these ladies have my measurements from earlier, and I would very much like a simple gown just in the silk, if there is enough. Thank you." She looked pleadingly as Mrs Bryson who smiled in return before speaking over her head to her aunt about pleating and underskirts and ensured her that both dresses would be ready in time, as long as they started straight away.

Her mornings exertions and two glasses of sherry having wearied the dame, she agreed and order was soon restored to the house.

"I will take a little rest, Katherine. But a drive this afternoon would be quite pleasant."

"Certainly aunt, I will arrange it."

Peace embraced the house and Kitty escaped to the library. Her intention had been to finished this dratted letter, but realised there was a pile of correspondence, cards and newspapers waiting for her. Sighing, she set to work.

That evening's card party was a huge success. Not only was Aunt Charlotte flush with success to the tune of five guineas, but Kitty had managed to have a conversation over a game of piquet with Lady Harriet Blair.

The lady was both a lover of cards and not beyond adding up points in her favour. Thus, she often found it hard to find a partner among her close acquaintance so was more than happy when Kitty sought her out. The reason was that as Kitty had observed her other vice was gossip.

"I see that Mrs Bottomley is not here tonight."

"As expected; her darling grandson's funeral was yesterday."

"Oh yes indeed. Has anything been discovered about the circumstances of his death?"

"Nothing further, and I doubt Harriet will ever see her pearls again or would want to."

"Was the funeral in Folkestone?"

"Oh no dear, Rochester."

"Isn't that in Kent?"

"Quite so, oh I seem to have won?"

In her room, later that night, Kitty finally finished the letter to her father. Reading it through, it made her sound quite the blue stocking with her detailed description of St Paul's.

 unt Charlotte was quite amenable to a visit to St
 Paul's. Still buoyed up by her winnings on the journey
home, the idea seemed quite excellent. But in the cold light of
day her usual church and its later services appealed more. So, it
was then that Poppy and Kitty sallied forth alone into the quiet
London streets. Not that London was ever quiet but very few
of their acquaintance would be at matins.

However, Kitty's goal was not salvation but a chance to spy
out Mr Bostock.

Somewhat surprised, she and Poppy found themselves not
in the main cathedral but in the Morning Chapel. Smaller and
incredibly beautiful, it reminded Kitty of home, and the service
with its familiar responses soothed and comforted her.
However, she became aware of Poppy's elbow in her side as
they stood to sing along with the choir. Looking up from her
hymnal she saw Bostock amid the other adult choristers. So, he
had not been a figment of her imagination. Now she was no
longer able to concentrate on the service. Under cover of the
next hymn she asked Poppy. "Did you get the message to
Clarky?"

"For goodness sake, yes, miss," came the hissed reply.

She had charged Poppy with finding the address of Mr Bostock from the choristers. While she had been sorting through the exquisite fabrics, Poppy had found her way to Cheapside with the aid of Clara, one of the housemaids. Together they had found one of the boys loitering near a pot house and with the incentive of a fresh pie and a shilling engaged him to show them where Mr Bostock lodged. A further shilling was dispensed to ensure his silence, with the promise of more if he heard that the man was leaving the area. Poppy and Clara both thought she had overpaid but Kitty, with Martha Hackett still fresh in her mind, had been quite insistent on the amount.

It was during the Creed that realisation struck. As the choir was required at matins, this was the ideal time to search the man's rooms. Cursing herself for her stupidity, her common sense kicked in to say that she was hardly suited to wandering through Cheapside and searching a clergyman's rooms in broad daylight.

The problem now lay with Kitty's curiosity. She was unlikely to see Mr Gregory before the ball and how was she to know if they had followed up on her clues when even she had not seen them for what they were.

She was now very eager to leave and even keener that Mr Bostock should not recognise her. There was no reason for him to think that she was on his trail, but his guilty conscience may have made him overly suspicious of even the slightest coincidence. But she was trapped. The size of the chapel made it impossible for them to leave now without creating a stir and she didn't know whether the choir would process to the main door with the clergy or stay in their place. There was nothing for it, she would just have to brazen it out.

Kitty schooled herself to think about everything she had said to Mr Bostock at The Towers. They had only met that once over dinner, where they had both been on sufferance. She could not remember if they had had any conversation whatsoever.

Lost in her thoughts, she realised that the congregation was standing and that the tide of cassocks and surplices had already passed her.

The sunlight streamed in from outside, casting shadow on those in the doorway. As they waited for their carriage to pull up, a voice hailed her,

"Miss Lucas?"

Turning she caught sight of Mr Bostock beaming at her in full chorister's ensemble.

"It is Miss Lucas, is it not? Mr Bostock. We met at The Towers at Easter?" he prompted.

"Why indeed, Mr Bostock. I am pleased to see you so well after your accident. Are you quite recovered?"

"Thank you, yes."

"But you left Epsom?"

"Yes, the doctor suggested sea air so I have been spending some time with an old university friend. I recently found a post at the cathedral here."

"How are you finding it?"

"Very different but I am sure I will become accustomed to it. And you, Miss Lucas, have you a position in London?"

"Yes, I am a companion to an elderly lady who had a fancy to come to matins, but then at the last minute cried off. I am here as her proxy. It is quite a magnificent building."

"It is. I would be happy to give you a tour?"

"Thank you, Mr Bostock but the carriage… and I am expected back. On this occasion …"

"I will not take no for an answer. At least let me show you the dome. The carriages take for ever and if you leave your maid here she can instruct the carriage to meet us at the South Transept."

Conscious that people were starting to look and not wanting to make a scene, she smiled her agreement and took the man's proffered arm. She looked what she hoped was a warning to Poppy and the young girl scurried out through the crowds of worshippers.

Mr Bostock was charming and informed and she began to relax.

"Would you like to see the library?"

"I did not know there was a library here."

He gave an enthusiastic nod. "Oh yes, and quite a history it has too. If you are interested in ecclesiastical tracts."

"It maybe heresy sir, but it is not my first choice of reading matter. In fact, I recently discovered a paper called Lloyd's List and have found it quite fascinating."

"Fascinating in what way? Ah, we're here."

She followed his outstretched arm up towards the dome and soon both were leaning back to take in the details. He moved closer to her to point out the whispering, stone and golden galleries. She made appreciative noises about the facts and figures he gave but she became increasingly conscious that he was now putting his arm on her shoulder ostensibly to guide her view. She could smell him; an odour of badly aired clothing, sweat and a rather awful pomade. She could also hear that his breathing was becoming more pronounced. She took a small step away and faced him, rubbing her neck.

"Over 500 steps appears to be excessive. And it certainly gives one a crick in the neck. But you have been too generous with your time and I must return the carriage."

He made her a bow and threaded her arm into the crook of his own and escorted her to the door patting her hand as he did so.

"It is difficult when one is well-educated but always at the beck and call of an indifferent employer."

As they entered the gloom of the transept he stopped,

turned towards her and stroked her hand. She was mortified should anyone see and made to walk on pulling her arm from his. She was unfamiliar with the door and fumbled with the mechanism. He reached her in a step and pressed himself her up against the door. He inhaled her hair deeply before running a finger down her arm to find and turn the handle before stepping back to bring the door towards them.

Light flooded in and she blinked.

"And I believe this is your carriage waiting."

He was all smiles and composure, and walked by her side to the vehicle drawing her attention to the Roman ruins reportedly running beneath them. His bow and goodbye were kind and charming, and Kitty was flummoxed. Did she imagine what happened? Had she misinterpreted his actions and intentions? She hoped that her face showed none of these emotions.

As she was being handed up into the carriage, she turned:

"Mr Bostock this has most interesting and informative, thank you."

"Miss Lucas, a pleasure and I hope to see you again soon. At evensong perhaps."

She smiled and took her seat. Oh lord, perhaps he had seen her the other times she had been to the cathedral and he mistook it for romantic interest on her part.

"What was all that about then?" asked Poppy.

"I think he believes I am enamoured of him."

Poppy laughed loudly but Kitty refused to see the humour in it. For a few minutes she had felt herself isolated and vulnerable, and neither were feelings she relished.

What unsettled her was that she had seen him as a thief and possibly a murderer rather than a lecher. She must have been at fault. Perhaps he thought that that was what she wanted? Had she wanted it? Had she tempted him? Unbidden, she remembered the words of a curate who had worked in her father's parish when she was small. He talked about crusades and smiting evil. He railed about the sins of the flesh and the weakness and carnal nature of woman. His eyes flashed and his spittle hit her there on the front pew.

Then she remembered Mrs Dorney, their old housekeeper, stroking her hair as she recounted her fears.

"Remember, sweetling," she had said, "People is people. There are good ones and bad ones but most are a mixture of the two. There are big wrongs like stealing Mrs Mackey's calf or little ones like taking an apple from the orchard or pulling hair. But the biggest wrongs are seeing evil all around God's world rather than the good he put into it, telling young girls that they are to blame for what others think and do and using their position to excise their own bad thoughts."

It was the biggest speech Mrs Dorney ever made and father had dispensed with the services of his crusading curate shortly after.

Kitty wanted to stay hidden and safe and the weather conspired with her as the sunshine of the morning did not persist and the rest of the day she planned to spend reading sermons, of which Mr Elliot seemed to have acquired an inordinate amount. When Kitty had mentioned it her aunt had laughed,

"He bought them Katherine but never read any. And I am not about to start. Pass the deck of cards dear. "

Thus, four games of piquet dispelled her devils and she began to see Mr Bostock as the opportunist and blackguard he so obviously was. But they had no proof. True, she thought Mr Gregory might have searched his lodgings but she had no certainty that he had or that he would share his findings with her. There was only one thing for it.

Never one to stay out of society for a whole day, evening saw her aunt suggesting evensong but Kitty had a plan. Feigning a headache, she asked to be excused and asked that she may rest and perhaps take a stroll instead. Having noted her niece being out of sorts, her aunt agreed to both plans.

Wearing the most countrified clothes in their wardrobes, Kitty and Poppy strolled towards the gardens. When out of sight of the house they hailed a cab and Poppy gave their destination.

Having paid the driver off, they found themselves a couple of streets away from Mr Bostock's lodgings.

The houses were closer together, greenery was in short supply but the pavements were swept and the houses and streets were respectable, with clean windows and polished brasses.

"What if Mr Bostock is 'ere, Miss."

"He will be at evensong. It is the perfect opportunity."

Neither girl looked out of place but its respectability could be a problem when it came to gaining entry. Walking arm-in-arm as two companions would they approached their target. Kitty thought a plan would come to her but, so far, she had nothing and they walked to the end of the road. With the services of a street cleaner they crossed the road and returned along the other side, when out of the door came a figure Kitty recognised. She had last seen him outside an abandoned mill within which he had then seen fit to place her.

"We need to follow him."

"Who?"

"Him, that man coming out of the house. He put John, Patrick and myself in the mill. Come on."

"What about the house ..."

"I want to see where he goes. We might not get another chance. Come on."

Kitty hoped that he would not be going into somewhere they could not follow. And that they would not lose their bearings. After a couple of turns he entered an inn.

"You can't go in there, Miss."

"I have been in many inns, Kitty."

"Not like this one and he might see you. He don't know me. Read this sign 'ere and don't talk to no one."

With that she disappeared inside and Kitty was left to peruse a poster advertising the delights of a travelling circus. Intrigued by the number of grotesques they had advertised, she was caught unawares by Poppy barging her along the street and around the corner.

"Walk, miss, and don't look worried."

"I am not worried."

"Good then."

"Should I be worried?"

"'Course not, miss."

When they had cleared the area they managed to hail a cab, which was told to drop them at the park near Hanover Square.

"What is going on, Poppy? Did he see you?"

"Nah, but I almost gave the game away by bumping into 'im. 'E was asking about two seats on the stage to Dover and I wanted a closer listen."

The girl seemed flushed and her studied speech had melted into a hotchpotch of dialects picked up from the scores of servants' halls she had visited since they came to London.

"Poppy, are you alright?"

"Yeh, I just pretended to be Miss Watkins, she could freeze a fireball if she wanted wiv one of 'er looks."

"Poppy, perhaps I did wrong to bring you away from Epsom."

"Never, miss. I woulda never seen all this or met so many people. Never say that, miss. Ever."

"Alright Poppy. When did he want to go to Dover?"

"First thing in the morning, miss."

"Let me think."

They began to stroll around the small park in silence,

interspersed by Kitty's questions. "Did he give any name? Where does the coach leave from?"

As far as Kitty could determine, the two seats were for him and Mr Bostock, or one of the men and another boy who thought he was off on an adventure. She could go to the authorities, but really she had nothing in the way of evidence to a crime. Mr Gregory and Clarky could have found evidence, but she had no way of knowing if they had. She needed a carriage and was unsure if her funds would run to a fare to Dover without checking. Finishing their circuit, they returned home to find guests.

In the large drawing room sat Mr Gregory with her aunt. Both turned as she entered.

"Oh, you have a much better colour now, Katherine. Look who I found at church. I thought the heathen boy would have had more interesting ways of spending his Sunday."

"Thank you, aunt. I feel much better now too."

"Edward has been telling me a most frightful tale."

"Really?"

"Yes, it is all about a young curate who has been encouraging young boys to leave home for adventure at sea."

"I agree it could be a shock to their parents, but frightful?"

"Yes, it appears they steal from their family to fund their adventure and then disappear never to be seen again."

"I agree, it is frightful aunt. And have the authorities not been alerted, Mr Gregory?"

To those who didn't know her the slight flush might be down to the fresh air she had recently enjoyed. To Kitty feeling herself colour, she wasn't so sure as to the cause. Seeing Mr Gregory all unprepared had had a curious effect on her, while hearing her aunt discuss the horrors endured by the boys as if it was just one other piece of society gossip made her feel slightly nauseous.

Just as she was about to say something that she would

regret, she caught sight of a glint of ice and steel in Mr Gregory's eye and with a pride in her own self-possession picked up the proffered tea cup with a steady hand.

"Is this tea, aunt?"

"I know, dear, but since Miss Carmichael heard Reverend Edgar preach, I am loath to serve anything stronger on a Sunday."

"Is she visiting us?"

"No, but last Sunday evening I definitely heard her sniffing for alcohol behind me in church and I will not be sniffed at!"

Feeling that the day could hardly get any stranger, she turned all smiles to their visitor.

"So, Mr Gregory what are the authorities going to do?"

At times, Kitty thought her aunt's actions could be seen as whimsy permissible by someone of her advanced years. Yet dim recollections of conversations between her parents made her think that the passing of time had little to do with it. All that Kitty knew now was that she was sitting in a carriage with her aunt, Poppy and Watkins; all bound for Dover.

Yesterday afternoon with cup paused between saucer and lips, she had heard Mr Gregory explain to her aunt that both the office of the Earl of Liverpool and Prince Regent had been informed about the murder of William Bottomley and Mr Bostock's diabolical scheme.

"So madame, I have a request. May I borrow your companion in the role of governess to travel with me to Dover."

"Dover?"

"Yes, ma'am. We have reasons to believe that another young boy is in danger and to prevent scandal I would ask for Miss Lucas to accompany me there and to escort him home. She is known to the boy and his family. She will of course be in no danger."

"While I appreciate the subterfuge, Mr Gregory, this will not do. Why would you need a governess? What scandal? This man is a murderer and the authorities should arrest him post haste. For my niece to accompany you would be quite unsuitable as well you know."

He turned to face the fireplace and silence filled the room. Kitty could hear the odd creak as unseen servants managed the minutiae of day-to-day living. Somewhere off a clock chimed, a carriage lumbered past and Kitty realised that she had stopped breathing.

"Aunt, let me tell you the story of a boy called Patrick…"

When the story reached the mill, her aunt's face blanched. Mr Gregory rang for brandy. With her aunt thus fortified, Kitty continued.

"This man has booked passage to Dover for tomorrow. If we follow him we may find out more and stop another child's youthful folly," finished Kitty.

"Unfortunately," said Mr Gregory, "I have a little more information to add. Patrick's uncle has been advised by his son that travelling to the continent now would be better than waiting until the autumn and the less favourable crossing conditions. He uses Patrick's condition as an excuse and his availability to help with the travel arrangements as additional inducements for an early departure. He has also found an old university friend of his to act as tutor."

Her aunt passed her the brandy glass.

"Edward, I have developed a sudden desire to travel. I am not getting any younger and the recent unpleasantness across the channel has tempered by wanderlust. However, now everything is settled I would like to visit Italy. France no longer holds kind memories but I think Kitty should see Venice. Not Rome, too many ruins and priests. Would you be so good as to accompany us to Dover? Would tomorrow be convenient? Excellent."

And with that she swept out of the room and turned the house upside down with her orders and commands. Soon all was bustle and hustle.

In the drawing room all remained quiet. Kitty and Mr Gregory turned to face each other.

"You have been busy, Miss Lucas."

"We both have, sir."

"Surely this is a rash move on the Reverend's part."

"I believe our combined efforts have forced his hand," she said. "I was wondering how to contrive to get to Dover tomorrow."

"Why doesn't that surprise me?"

"I thought you would be … cross."

He moved towards her and took her hand. Raising it to his lips, he smiled.

"That boat has sailed, Kitty." Bowing, he let go her hand but paused at the door. "*A demain, ma petite.*"

As to be expected, the demands of ordering the household upside down had taken their toll of her aunt and she now slept surrounded by cushions, rugs and a cooled hot brick.

Atop the box was her usual driver accompanied by Clarky in new livery. The plan was that Mr Gregory would meet them outside Maidstone, where they would break their journey and change horses.

Kitty found herself in something of a quandary; they were moving but she didn't feel that she was doing anything. Her thoughts were drawn to Mr Gregory. He only told her what he wanted her to know, which was always frustrating. He hadn't really taken much notice of her until yesterday and his attentions were flattering but she didn't trust them, and certainly not her response to them, which she had admonished herself about into the small hours.

Had he revealed too much of himself earlier and was trying to deflect further enquiry? Her eyelids closed. Did she trust him? What was he doing now? She only had his word for the information about Patrick, she hadn't heard from Bath herself. Was he just getting her out of the way? But why? She dozed.

A blast of fresh air woke her as it broke through the haze of warm bodies too heavily clothed. The Red Lion lay before them. Fresh white walls and flowers peeping out between the kerbstones proclaimed their freedom from London. As she stepped down into the sunshine she saw a pleasant town closing down for the day and she was suddenly overwhelmed with homesickness.

Aunt Charlotte was bustled inside with the two maids following in her wake. Her aunt demanded her room and dinner in it, while the landlord pointed out the features of his establishment including the private parlour. Kitty quietly slipped inside and took up residence. A small fire was lit and she was pleased to see it as the room was north facing and cool despite the good weather.

A small table in the window was equipped with paper and a drawer hid pen and ink. She set to on a letter home. So engrossed was she that Kitty barely noticed an oil lamp brought into the gathering gloom and completely failed to acknowledge Poppy enquiring if she needed anything. Enticing smells of hot gammon pulled her back to the present, as the table was laid for dinner and additional candles added. Finishing her letter, sealing and addressing it carefully she put it on the dresser for the landlord to post. Straightening her back she faced the fire and noticed Mr Gregory reading there.

"I am sorry, sir, I did not notice your arrival."

"I was trying not to disturb you. Are you ready to eat?"

She knew that she should have felt at the very least embarrassed and uncomfortable in such an unorthodox setting; eating with a man she was not related to and on her own. But she didn't and it amused her a little when he added for the benefit of the servants,

"Wine, cousin?"

Soon they were on their own and addressing their meal. The fare was good and both had keen appetites.

The quietness of the setting was initially pleasant and comfortable but soon Kitty could feel the questions and her frustration building within.

"I was surprised to see you here," she said.

He frowned. "Why? This is what we arranged."

"Do you have a sailing time?"

"Yes, as do you Miss Lucas. I'm sure you are still perusing Lloyds' admirable publication."

She said nothing for a moment,

"Is saving Patrick enough?"

He placed his cutlery on his plate. "No, we need something more permanent."

"Like a confession?"

"Like a confession. I believe he and his father, and even yours, would say it is good for the soul."

"That will not be easy," she said, dabbing her mouth delicately with a napkin.

"No."

"Perhaps we should just confront them with the facts and see what happens?"

"That might work," he said

"It is not much of a plan."

He frowned. "No."

"Is there anything else I need to know?" Kitty asked, growing more irritated at his taciturn responses.

"No."

Pushing her chair from the table, she stood: "Then I will bid you goodnight, sir."

"Goodnight."

If Miss Katherine Lucas was a young lady who flounced, then her departure from the room would have been described in just such a way.

The next morning, they were greeted by a new carriage pulled by four fresh horses. Their carriage and driver plus Watkins were to await their return – later today or tomorrow. The new driver togged up in appropriate livery was their very own Mr Gregory. Aunt Charlotte choose not to look as she was handed into the carriage by the landlord.

The sedate pace for the high street soon changed as the horses were given their heads and the passengers made use of the leather straps. Aunt Charlotte's eyes were bright.

"Very well sprung, this conveyance. Don't you agree?"

"It shifts a bit ma'am," replied Poppy gripping the strap and pressing her lips together tightly

"A landau and four-in-hand. I am thinking speed is important today, aunt."

A jolt sent the three women tumbling, a curse was heard from above and the speed slackened.

"Our driver is very experienced, dear Kitty."

"New, ma'am?"

"Yes, but he came recommended."

"What is he called?" said Kitty.

"Peters."

"He looked familiar?"

"Can't say I noticed."

Poppy had turned from white to grey and not back to white. Kitty handed her Aunt Charlotte's smelling salts. She was thanked with a brave smile before Poppy returned her determined gaze to the window and the outside world.

"Aunt, why is Mr Gregory dressed as a coachman?"

"I have no idea. But he will have his reasons. Gentlemen like to have their fun you know."

They soon settled into a desultory conversation about the changing countryside and weather. As they crossed the Downs the clouds darkened but the rain seemed a way off. Kitty would have longed to have stretched her legs when they changed horses but it seemed that everything was done at top speed and only once did Aunt Charlotte and Kitty insist that they stop for longer. When they returned, a basket of food was sitting in the carriage next to a sleeping Poppy.

Dusty and with his mouth covered, Mr Gregory helped them into the carriage.

"No more stops to Dover now ladies. Let's hope we beat the weather."

"How..." But her question remained unasked as he climbed on top and Kitty was left to shut the door as they eased out of the inn and onto the open road.

The sea was now to their right and it looked dark and unwelcoming. But the road was well managed and they picked up speed again. Kitty was tempted to wake Poppy so she could see the Channel but the young girl's pallor convinced Kitty to let her sleep. Aunt Charlotte pointed out the obvious as they passed through Folkestone and over the Hoe towards Dover interspersed with tales of the previous journeys of her youth. Scoundrels and dashing young men seemed to come up a lot, but today was not the day for digging deeper.

Their pace was now pedestrian and the change in rhythm woke Kitty whose travel woes were replaced by her amazement at the sights before her as well as the smells and cawing of the seagulls.

It was early afternoon when they stepped down from the carriage and the first fat raindrops hit Kitty's gloved hand as she was handed down to stand before the Ship Inn.

Poppy all of a sudden came to and began ordering boxes

and trunks to be taken inside. Aunt Charlotte used her style and presence, plus a handful of coins, to convince the landlord of their previous booking, so Kitty was left with *Peters*.

"Righto Miss, Clarky and me will make for our own barracks and compliments of Mr Gregory he will present himself after he has checked the sailing times."

"Oh. Yes, thank you, Peters. Excellent driving by the way."

"Very kind, miss, I'm sure."

The Ship Inn was a melting pot of the respectable, desperate, needy and unscrupulous, while posters on the walls detailed the stage coach times and public auctions. Kitty trotted after her aunt to a bedroom-cum-sitting room. Large and clean, the windows faced the harbour where vessels quiet and still berthed next to others a hive of endeavour.

"Now what?" asked Poppy.

"Mr Gregory is finding information on the Persephone."

"Excellent, well I'm going to sleep." And with that her aunt closed her eyes.

"Our cue to discover the sights of Dover."

"Really, miss?"

"Really, Poppy."

However, in this they were thwarted by the rain which was now coming down like stair-rods; washing debris towards the harbour and sending all but the most hardy sailor clad in oilskins for the nearest shelter. Places offering libation where obviously popular and the Ship Inn was noisy and jolly. Avoiding the public areas, Poppy and Kitty decided to reconnoitre the hotel for signs of Patrick and his guardian.

Poppy was all for heading downstairs and asking the servants.

"Poppy. this is not the same as your inn or London, I feel we might be out of our depth."

"What d'ya mean, miss."

"We do not have the right experience for this."

"Oh, miss, when has that ever stopped us, eh?" Smiling, she skipped downstairs leaving Kitty with a 'take care' still on her lips.

Kitty took a flight of stairs up and ambled along the corridor looking for nothing and anything. Having made that circuit, she returned to the floor with their room before descending to the more public floor of dining halls where she found a waiting room.

Smiling an apology as she walked around a lady surrounded by boxes, she made a show of looking at the chalked messages and sailing information while carefully moving in between chairs and other seekers of information. She was just working her way through the timetable of tides when she heard a voice she recognised.

"Uncle, it is still raining. I'll run and get the umbrellas."

Keeping her eyes cast down, she turned to see Patrick make for the stairs while two reverend gentlemen talked, both with their backs to her.

Her first thought was to follow him but was too slow as almost immediately Patrick returned and all three set off. Making note of their direction, she returned to the room. Her aunt was now ensconced in dressing gown, cap and enjoying a cup of hot chocolate while reading her bible.

"Aunt, would you mind if I went out, I have a mind to buy a book for the journey."

"An excellent idea, I believe the Beyle and Goethe would be useful. Do you prefer the French or the German?"

"I will see what they have, aunt. Can I acquire anything else?"

"More smelling salts, especially if all forms of travel make your Foster unwell."

"We are not really going abroad, aunt."

"We will see, we will see." And on such gnomic utterances she closed her eyes and smiled serenely.

Donning hat and coat and clutching an umbrella, Kitty made for the door. Standing there and similarly dressed was Poppy.

"Lady Charlotte is resting and I have some small purchases to make. Shall we?"

"Yes, miss. Master Patrick and his companions are using Rooms 32 and 31, miss."

"Good work Poppy. They have just left."

"We could check their rooms!"

"What for? Patrick is with them and seems in good spirits." But seeing Poppy's downcast expression, added: "But it is useful to know and it may yet prove vital information."

As she pulled the door closed, she thought she heard another door close simultaneously. Glancing along the corridor she saw nothing, but her unease remained.

Kitty decided she liked Dover; it was exotic and familiar all at the same time. The bookshop was typical of its kind; a mixture of glue and leather, which offered promise and surprise behind uncut pages. She dutifully enquired after travel guides and was presented with a selection of tomes scribed by travellers and tutors to this lordling or that so she picked one at random by a Henry Holland.

Before returning to the Ship she popped into the chemists - another of her favourite establishments, from the polished mahogany to the smells of camphor and oil. The colours in the glass jars were intriguing and she remembered when she first saw leeches writhing just like those above the young shop assistant's head. The shop was busy so Kitty was left to peruse the display of pre-prepared remedies for *mal de mer*. One of the voices seemed familiar and concentrating on the display before her she soon matched it to her memory of Mr Bostock. Images of St Paul's returned to her and she found it impossible to face him again.

"Poppy, the man being served. Describe him to me," she hissed.

"Can't really see 'im. Black vicar garb and a big flat hat."

"Fine. Now look at these and don't turn around."

"What was he buying?"

"White powder. Don't know what but the pharmacist came out for it."

The flurry of customers thinned before too long and Kitty chose a tincture and some lavender water both favoured said the pharmacist's apprentice for their restorative properties. Fumbling for the coins and offering the lad the full benefit of her smile, she said:

"Was that Mr Bostock buying a draft? I know he uses it for his indigestion?"

"The reverend gentleman, miss? Yes, he was making his own remedy while he was abroad and just checking the quantities, miss, you don't want to get the arsenic and limestone the wrong way round," he said, giving a brisk nod of his head to acknowledge the heavy responsibility his young shoulders bore.

"Certainly not, but then he is a very careful man.

"Good day, miss and safe journey."

There was more activity around the harbour wall, so Kitty and Poppy made for the hotel to, hopefully, news of the Persephone. As they neared the building they saw Mr Gregory enter so they picked up their pace.

Almost immediately Patrick, Reverend Templeton-Hughes and another clerical gentlemen turned the corner and were met at the steps to the building by Mr Bostock. Kitty slowed and watched mesmerised as he shook hands with the younger man before being introduced to the elder. A package was passed, an entreaty to enter the hotel offered and declined before farewells were taken. It was then with horror that Kitty realised Mr Bostock was headed her way. Pushing Poppy in front of her she entered the nearest shop.

The chandlers was yet another assault on her senses intensified by the gloom which surrounded them. However, her eyes soon adjusted and she made her way to the archetypal old sea dog who was sitting behind the counter. He looked as though he had come straight out of a story; it brought a smile to her face. He responded with a version of his own but without teeth.

"Arfternon missus. A nice change to my usual customers. What brings you 'ere?"

Thinking quickly Kitty said: "A young friend of ours is sailing today so we thought to buy him something as a memento, but something that was useful."

"A lad be it?"

"Yes, fourteen."

"Then I've just the thing."

And he lifted down a knife with a heavy horn handle.

"I think that is just the thing, but maybe a little large for him at present."

He looked thoughtful for a moment and pulled a box from under the counter. Inside were a selection of murderous objects.

"Oh my!"

He delicately extracted a knife with a narrow and pointed blade which he folded into a stag horn handle. The top was shaped like a fishtail which gave it a whimsical feel.

"French. And as it folds it keeps the sharp bits away from young fingers."

"I think that is just the thing, but I am not sure if my funds will run to it."

Poppy moved away to check both the window display and the street.

The glint of battle reached the old man's eyes and they fell to haggling. Kitty spent more than she wanted on this unwanted purchase but as it was half of what he had been asking she felt fairly pleased with herself. The horn handle felt strong and warm and the knife was well balanced, or so the old man had said. It now rested in her reticule with her bottles of remedies.

As they entered Aunt Charlotte's room Mr Gregory was sipping a glass of beer and Clarky was pouring red liquid into a glass for her aunt.

"An elder wine for my niece, too."

"No thank you. Why elder wine?"

"It is very fortifying before a sea voyage." Her aunt took a sip and gave a satisfied nod.

"What sea voyage?"

"The Persephone leaves on the first tide tomorrow," explained Mr Gregory.

"But they are all here: Patrick both Hughes-Templetons."

"Templeton-Hughes."

"They have rooms here, and they have poison and Bostock."

She sat down, removed her coat and gloves from Clarky, then started the explanation.

"But it still can all be explained," said Mr Gregory, now fully restored to his stylish self after his role as carriage driver. "Bostock was helping out a friend who has stomach problems and up to now all the boys have drowned not been poisoned. We have no proof."

Kitty grimaced. "I thought we were going for a confrontation and confession?"

"Where?"

"Here."

"And how?"

"We could invite them to dinner," offered her aunt.

Mr Gregory's handsome forehead creased with thought.

"And what about Bostock and the other big fellow? Perhaps they are coming by stage as you thought, Miss Lucas?"

"Musta done, sir," Poppy entered slightly out of breath and leant on the door behind her. "'Cos the big man is dawnstairs."

Clarky slipped out.

According to Poppy, the man downstairs was called Collins, and he was to act as gentleman's gentleman to all the Templeton-Hughes until they reached Calais. Then he'd be travelling with the younger man to Germany while father and nephew journeyed to Italy and Greece. They would be picking up a man to act as guide in Calais, a friend of the young Reverend called Mr Bostock.

"Did this Collins recognise you?" asked Kitty.

"Na, thought I'd take the first step and ask him if we'd met before? Complained about being made to find out about stagecoaches when I knew we'd be travellin' by our own carriage. Explained that Lady Charlotte was a bit of a 'centric old coot. Sorry ma'am."

Aunt Charlotte gave an imperious nod of the head. "Apology accepted, this time."

"So why so complicated. Why isn't Bostock travelling with them now?" asked Kitty.

"'E says e's a companion to another young man on a different vessel but that task finishes when he is delivered to his family in Calais," added Clarky newly returned from the public bar and servant's hall.

"But that is a lie," cried Kitty. "We know he is employed at St Paul's and travelled to Dover with this Collins fellow only today or yesterday."

"But Edward," asked Lady Charlotte. "Why lie?"

"For an alibi," said Mr Gregory and Kitty in unison.

"So what vessel is he travelling on?" asked Lady Charlotte.

"They will all be on the Persephone – but the good Mr Bostock who is so good with young boys will be invisible," explained Mr Gregory.

"So that means something happen on the Persephone. Can we get onboard the boat?" asked Kitty.

Edward shook his head. "Not all of us, no. There are only two berths left."

"I thought…" began Lady Charlotte.

"No!"

"Then I will host a farewell dinner for Mr Gregory. Kitty, find the landlord of this establishment. Then contrive an invitation for the Templeton-Hughes. Off you go."

"But …"

Before she knew it, she was on the other side of the door. She walked downstairs and set about persuading the landlord that not only did her ladyship now want the room for the night, that they needed another two rooms and would be holding a private dinner in a private parlour for six. His concerns assuaged with promises of largesse and that with the bonus that no additional servants would be needed to serve the food as they had their own, he agreed.

All she had to do now was *bump* into the Templeton-Hughes party. As she had spent most of the afternoon avoiding this, it seemed a little unfair that they had now gone to ground. On her third circuit of the hotel, she spied Patrick bouncing a ball on a wall.

"Dear me, Patrick, what would Dr Parkin say?" Kitty exclaimed loudly. Very loudly.

The boy beamed with surprise. "Miss Lucas! How wonderful to see you. What are you doing here?"

"My aunt had a sudden whim to travel. Are you recovered?"

"Yes, thank you, as fit as a flea, so my uncle wants to show me Italy and Greece. He says it is the best way to study the classics."

"A Grand Tour then."

"Not really, my uncle was a tutor for someone many years ago and this is a good excuse for him to return."

"And you will be away for the winter, which is good news for your health too. Though I daresay John will miss you."

At that precise moment, Aunt Charlotte and Reverend Templeton-Hughes opened their respective doors recognising their relative's voice.

Introductions made and received, and recent unpleasantness not referred to, Lady Charlotte went on her charm offensive. Kitty was impressed and the Very Reverend Templeton-Hughes didn't stand a chance. How fortuitous that her favourite godson was travelling on the Persephone, too. They would be six for dinner.

Behind closed doors, Kitty asked. "Is Mr Gregory really your godson, aunt?"

"He could well be. I have so many I can't keep count. I just remember the ones I like."

Dinner was a success for Lady Charlotte and the elder Reverend. They had both travelled widely in their youth and traded stories like the veterans of old campaigns. Patrick was politely bored but tucked into the quite excellent food.

For the rest of the party it was an intricate dance. Clarky and Collins circled each other like prize fighters with Poppy on her best behaviour and the picture of surprised innocence. Kitty tried to reproduce Poppy's performance while Mr

Gregory and the younger Reverend toyed with the food and nimbly sidestepped questions. It was all rather a strain. No one mentioned Mr Bostock.

"Do you travel often?"

"Do you have a parish at the moment?"

"What do you fancy for the Derby?"

"I believe you know my friends the Bottomleys." It was Kitty's turn. "It was quite horrific what happened to them. He was found quite close to here, wasn't he, aunt?"

"Yes, Folkestone."

"I was sorry to hear about the loss of your brother and his wife last year," added Mr Gregory.

"Thank you. It was a great shock. As a family we have all been keen sailors. For Patrick and myself I think the journey will be quite telling. I am grateful Claude can accompany us, he has no such fears."

"How terrible. Will you stay below decks?"

"Patrick, you must stay close to your uncle when onboard. The weather report is for fog tomorrow."

"Don't worry, Miss Lucas, I will keep a keen eye on my cousin,"

"I am sure you will."

Mr Gregory entered the fray: "And Miss Lucas, I will be aboard so can aid Mr Templeton-Huges with his task.""I wouldn't want to put you to any trouble," countered Claude."No trouble, I assure you."

Checking of watches was the precursor to the preparation for leaving. Patrick was yawning openly but Kitty insisted that he come upstairs as she had a little gift for him.

Lady Charlotte insisted they use her carriage to transport them and soon all the men were aboard. There was much reordering of boxes to her liking and good wishes plus vague plans to meet in Rome or Naples.

Patrick came bounding down stairs and the only place available was next to Clarky and Collins.

Upstairs at The Ship a young boy woke with a start and looked into Poppy's eyes.

"You're staying on dry land young Patrick. We're not losing you again! Not get dressed in these nice new clothes, Lady Catherine wants a word."

# ALL'S WELL THAT ...

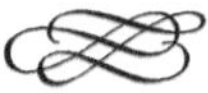

Truly it was Mr Gregory's fault as he gave her the idea by dressing up as Peters. Everyone was too preoccupied trying to score points or concentrating on their stomach, to notice the boy falling asleep in their midst thanks to some poppy juice in his cordial. There had been no confrontation, they had all proved cowards when faced with the charge of bad manners.

Innocent members of the party were oblivious, while others would be more on their guard or warned off. Kitty was not prepared to put Patrick in danger of losing his life, again. In her opinion, Claude and Bostock had a good plan with a back-up if needed. One old man and young boy, neither in the best of health, stood little chance. Bostock would be hiding on board ready for an accident to be manufactured, while supposedly on a different ship altogether. As far as Kitty was concerned there were far too many unknowns for Patrick to be anywhere near. So wearing his clothes and fingering the present she had bought for him, she played the role of young lad dressed up against the night air in a thick coat, hat and scarf.

There was a general but orderly chaos at the dockside as goods and people were being loaded. Uncle Geraint insisted on bed for his nephew while he walked off some of his excellent repast. Alone in the cabin she was feigning sleep with her face to the bulkhead when the uncle returned. Determined to stay awake, before long the gentle swaying of the boat lulled her to sleep.

She was wakened by retching coming from the bunk next to her. After a while the door opened and Claude entered. Ministering quietly to his father, he insisted he drink a tincture to stop the sickness. Probably the very one she had bought in Dover. Gentle snores replaced the retching and Claude tiptoed from the room. Dressing quickly, she went on deck making sure she had coat, hat and scarf Just as well as she was met by a bank of fog. Bells sounded, and she knew it meant a time but couldn't remember what. It was an unpleasant night, but she felt less trapped and more in control of her fate on deck rather than below it.

Her plan, such as it was, was to stay out of sight until she could find Clarky or Mr Gregory. If all else failed, she would confess to the captain and be kept as a stowaway until Calais. All she had to do was to avoid both the Templeton-Hugheses, as well as Messrs Collins and Bostock. Well, she never said it was a good plan.

She found a small space under a set of stairs and hunkered down, wrapping coat and scarf around herself, Kitty became increasingly concerned about the murmurings in her gut. She would just sit very still and look straight ahead. She had caught a movement out of the corner of her eye as she moved in search of her hidey hole, but it was probably just a trick of the night.

After a while the fog lightened with the dawn. Shapes were moving about the decks, some with purpose, some without. Shrouds were opened as the wind picked up and then her stomach began its gymnastics proper. She saw servants rushing below decks with covered buckets. Others retched over the side while the sailors mocked and laughed. She became aware of three men walking slowly and separately around the deck as an enveloping fog continued to roll in.

All were buttoned up against the cold and damp and with the poor visibility, they could be anyone. apart. It soon became apparent that her need to be sick was becoming all consuming. If she could time it carefully perhaps she could slip to the side and relieve herself before returning in safety to her retreat.

More bells and then a gong. The smell of food implied a meal of some sort and the deck thinned of its few inhabitants. She tentatively made her way to the rail loosening her scarf as she went. Her legs were unsteady but she was intent and, despite the unpleasantness of the process, her relief was enormous. The wind blew away some of the cobwebs in her brain and the movement loosened the stiffened muscles that she had not even been aware of.

Just as she relaxed and stood up a hand covered her face and a voice whispered into her ear accompanied by a familiar but distasteful smell of hair oil.

"Time for a little dunking Master Templeton-Hughes."

It was Bostock. In the hours in her little hole she had been through what she would do in such a situation. As she ran through them all individually, the outcome had been the same. She was not strong enough so the unexpected would have to do. The movement had unsettled her hat her freed locks made Bostock pause and he loosened his grip enough to turn her around. Just then A breeze came up, clearly the fog enough for Bostock to recognise her. "What the devil… Why are you…? How did you …?"

She stood stock still, still held in his grip: "Of course you got Claudius to talk."

He smiled, which was something she had not expected. Could she brazen this out?

"Mr Bostock, what a surprise."

He didn't seem at all nonplussed. He fingered the colour of her coat and pulled her to him. He smelt her hair and moaned before moving both his hands to her throat. His hands were warm and smooth and she could feel the pressure of his fingers increase and relax as he spoke.

"Ahh, playing dress up Miss Lucas? I followed you from the old man's cabin, just waiting my time. But what fun we could have had, dear Miss Lucas. But you had to get involved in such a lovely scheme."

After initially stiffening, Kitty now made herself go limp. After counting to 20 and with all her will and strength she pushed down and back. She landed heavily on her bottom but she had broken his hold. Scrambling away to a neatly coiled rope further along the deck she suddenly found herself caught by the ankle.

Surprised but not incapacitated or concerned the man moved his hand up her left leg. She stretched for the rope but only managed to touch it with her fingertips as his sniggering laugh broke through the mist. Kitty could feel his hands stroke and caress her calf. She tried to kick out as she tasted bile in her mouth, then felt herself being hauled along the deck towards Bostock.

Finally, she found her voice and cried out in alarm, her hands scrambling on the deck for purchase as he encased her in his arms and dragged her to her knees. She had no doubt that she was going overboard. As he moved his grip to explore her chest with one hand, the other circled her neck as he nuzzled her hair and the wind dropped completely leaving her in an world of nightmare.

"The struggle is always my favourite part." The sound of his voice and touch of his hand appalled her. Kitty wanted so desperately to scream for help but couldn't – fear and disgust choked her. Bostock was too intent on possessing her body to utter anything more than a lustful grunt, which resulted in their struggle being a curiously muted affair and one which was swallowed from view by the thickening fog.

She found it all strangely impersonal. Her right arm was now free and she felt for the horn-handled knife in her pocket, flicking it open was not as easy as it had been in the shop. But as he pulled her to her feet it gave her the impetus she needed and she stabbed up deep into his thigh. Bostock roared in pain, his hands immediately went to the knife, freeing Kitty as she again staggered along the side of the ship finding a belaying pin. She tried to free it but her hands were slippery with blood. Her legs had no strength in them but she forced them to run and for the first time screamed before she ran straight into a wall with arms.

Looking up she saw Clarky. He lifted her out of the way as Bostock came down on her, blade first. He was stopped in his tracks by a bullet aimed centre forehead by Mr Gregory.

Back in the cabin and with her heart still pounding from her recent escape, Kitty cleaned herself up and settled the ailing old Reverend assuring him that the commotion was all a bit of a prank played by herself and Patrick, and that he was safe and well. These enquires alone seemed to exhaust him and he slept.

"Pass me my tincture, I am sure it will make me well soon."

Kitty went to pass it to him but she remembered who delivered it during the night and the white powders bought by Mr Bostock in Dover. The bottle slipped through her grasp. It didn't shatter but the contents were spread across the floorboard.

"I am so sorry, Reverend. I am sure there is a doctor on board. I will ask him to step in."

The herring gulls became more raucous as they made land and she wondered if she would be allowed ashore when they made Calais.

"Mr Gregory's compliments miss. He asked that you stay aboard and in the cabin with the old man," and with that Clarky passed her a parcel and left. The brown paper concealed a respectable looking dress, a little large perhaps but better than the breeches she was wearing.

Luckily for the old man, the young doctor who appeared sometime later at the cabin door had just graduated from Edinburgh and was a firm believer in fresh air and clean water. She liked his directness so asked him how you could test if something contained arsenic.

"There are tests. But none of them are reliable."

When passengers and cargo were off-loaded. There was a scratching at the door. She tiptoed passed the Reverend was sleeping fitfully calling out for his son from time to time. Outside was Clarky, putting her finger to her lips, she stepped outside pulling Patrick's coat around her.

"What is happening?"

"Mr Gregory says you're not here but in England with your aunt. Patrick and his uncle are unwell and under the doctor. The young Reverend has been persuaded to go ashore to find a suitable hostel for his father."

"Where is Mr Gregory?"

"Fixing passage for me and my niece on the next boat home."

"Your niece?"

"Yes miss, you miss."

Later that day she was on another boat as Miss Clark and homeward bound with her new uncle. Mr Gregory came to bid them farewell.

"I think Claude was going to take the chance that his father would continue to take the tonic and finally die by his own hand as a result of acute sickness when he was far away," she said.

Clarky agreed but Mr Gregory was more circumspect, "Again, Miss Lucas, there is no proof." She scrutinised him – there was no sign that less than a day ago he had killed a man in front of her eyes.

The old man was adamant that it was a just an extreme case of seasickness and bemoaned the fact that age had made him a poor sailor. Claude had found a most suitable hotel and a nurse for his father who was loath to return to England lest his illness start again. He would return in a day or two when he felt stronger, Claude would look after him.

No one said anything about Mr Bostock. When Kitty started to protest, Mr Gregory interrupted her. "He is dead, Miss Lucas. Remember Mr Bostock was never travelling on the Persephone but he won't be feeding on the daydreams of young lads anymore."

"But surely the Captain …"

"The Captain was happy that he was not going to be tied up in Calais while the case was investigated. Everyone agreed that it happened in British waters and the body and investigation would take place in England."

"Pricey?"

"It's only money, Miss Lucas."

"And Patrick and the old Reverend? Are they safe?"

"I will stay in France until he is well enough to travel. Claude is not stupid enough to try again so soon."

"So, you do believe me."

"Belief has never been the issue."

Nothing had been said when she had returned to Dover. Her aunt's carriage collected her from the Persephone and

Clarky drove them back to the Red Lion. But Lady Charlotte had hugged her hard and long.

"The scoundrel got what was coming to him. Do not give it another thought."

Within a week they were back in London. Patrick was staying with them until he could be reunited with his uncle, sadly laid low by a bad case of seasickness. Kitty told him nothing of Mr Bostock. To Poppy she was more forthcoming.

Almost as they entered the front door, fittings started for the Gregory Ball. Her aunt had her running all over London, it seemed, for this necessity or that. She felt strangely empty and unmoved by the quantities of fabric, lace and beads which surrounded both her and her aunt. She found she had few spare moments to think of either Mr Gregory or Mr Bostock. She had had a couple of night terrors on their journey back from Dover, but these nights she was so exhausted that she fell each night into a deep and dreamless sleep.

One of her joys, she found, was learning to play piquet - a necessity her aunt informed her if she was going to hold her own on the card tables.

"But aunt, I do not play cards for money." Kitty cut a three and her aunt a five.

"Of course not, dear, that would be inappropriate. But I do. You deal. Twelve cards for us both remember."

As the day approached she found herself nervous. Not for the ball, she would be a companion and was happy to be so. She would not shame her gracious and generous aunt in appearance or manner. Her fear was that he would talk to her or worse still would not.

Poppy had been practising, following the instructions of Watkins, when it came to hair and finer details. It transpired that any weakness or failing would be put down to the inexperience of her maid, not herself. Living up to other people's expectations was something that Kitty thought she had escaped. But a last look in the long glass showed a polished, demure lady of fashion. A view echoed by her aunt.

"Very nice, dear. We're ready, Garstang."

The evening was quite lovely. Kitty had never been in such a brightly lit building in her life. There were flowers in abundance, music, chatter and laughter. People were decked in their finest, a plethora of young girls looking hopeful and expectant with their mamas checking off prospective partners. All was elegance and quite beautiful.

A little part of Kitty wondered if this would have been her if her mother had lived. But mostly she liked being on the outside and looking on appreciatively. Following in Lady Charlotte's wake, they chose a location well away from the orchestra where she found a seat among friends. Kitty was sent for lemonade – nothing stronger would be served until later. Then she was at her leisure to observe the rich enjoying their riches while with half an eye watching for a dropped fan, or slipped shawl.

"Katherine dear, walk me to the card tables and then have a stroll and find me again in an hour. I'll be ready for some refreshments then."

"Certainly, aunt."

It was a warm night and the large windows were opened onto the lit lawns with lanterns hanging from the pergolas.

A familiar voice hailed her, "Would you care for some fresh air, Miss Lucas?"

He was behind her so she had mere moments to compose herself: "Mr Gregory. That would be pleasant but I must return shortly to my aunt."

"Of course, and I must pay my compliments."

Folding her fan and drawing her shawl around her shoulders they stepped down, side by side but not touching. Yet she was intensely aware of his body next to her.

"I trust that everything was well when you left France?"

"Claude is off on his travels now that Collins has joined him. Unfortunate how Collins fell and missed the sailing that night, Clarky couldn't account for it at all."

"And old Mr Templeton-Hughes?"

"Has forgone travelling. He feels that he needs to take the waters in Bath to fully restore him. Patrick is back at school and plans to spend the summer with John as originally planned."

They were alone now but continued to follow the path around the garden.

"So, he gets away with it?"

"He hasn't done anything to get away with."

"Do not split hairs with me. Kidnap, poisoning, murder…"

"No one was permanently harmed. No money changed hands and reputations are pristine."

"Oh yes. Reputations, don't let us forget those. He should hang."

"Be sensible. Hanging means a trial and washing laundry in public which would harm those already hurting. All proof and connection died with Bostock."

"You do agree people were harmed then. Where is the justice in all this?"

"Do you mean justice or retribution? Who would it help? Just those hungry for salacious gossip. Or worse, sedition. Think Katherine, this is the best option."

"Which means Claude sails into the sunset to start a new life, or until he returns to make another try for Patrick's fortune."

"And away from all the things that he loves – the best tailors, the best wines…"

"And gambling! Now who is being naïve. He will fall on his feet with new friends and no restraints of Society to keep him in check."

"We are not going to argue about this. It is done. A more important questions is, what next?"

His calm rational voice added to her frustration bringing her close to tears. She could feel them against her lashes so turned to look back at the glowing house. It was a most glorious view.

"Miss Lucas, it has been an honour."

She answered his bow with a demure curtsey. He turned to add something more, to see a small potted fern travelling towards him with devastating accuracy. Catching it with his left hand, he was at her side in two steps, circling her waist with his right he drew her to him.

Kitty reached up and pulled his head towards her. Melting into each other's embrace there was nothing tentative as their lips met. She felt his left hand on her neck as his right moved down bringing her closer. She arched her back, her whole body responding in a way which chased rational thought and consequences out of the window. As his tongue teased her lips apart, tasting her tongue with his own, she felt his body harden against hers. She was breathing hard now, her breasts squeezed against the confines of her dress and his chest. She gasped as her body undulated in a manner totally out of her control.

Suddenly he stopped kissing her. Loosening his grip and breathing heavily himself he stepped away. This time it was his turn to admire the view of the house. Rational thought returned, colouring her cheeks crimson and she thanked the dark for hiding her confusion. She turned her back while she recovered her equilibrium, his footsteps growing quieter as he disappeared into the night, leaving Kitty alone.

Clarky observed his quarry while he polished the brass light fittings, oiled the hinges, and washed salt from the wood. It was a needless precaution. the man's disdain for everything around him made subterfuge unnecessary. The passengers had been warned on boarding that this trip would be a rough one and all should stay in their cabins.

But Claude Templeton-Hughes had to return to England, to where his fortune was tied up in a young lad and an old infirm man. He had been unusually unfortunate at both track and table. All sorts of ill fortune had befell him since he left Calais from lame horses to stolen luggage. Collins had left him when the money ran out. It was time his luck changed.

As his target walked the lonely deck, Clarky watched; an accident waiting to happen…

# ABOUT THE AUTHOR

Pam Turnbull is a dedicated lover of history (having a university degree in the subject), and a dedicated reader of historical mystery books.

She has been a librarian, worked in a bookshop, organised book events, spent many years as an editor of computer and education magazines until she finally decided to become a teacher which she has been doing for the last sixteen years.

She lives in the North-West of England with her husband, dog, cat, lizards and giant snails - and grown-up children who always seem to come back. Not that she minds.

Pam has always told stories, often improvised, but she finally decided to use her knowledge of history and her skill with words to weave tales in the genre she loves to read.

# NEWSLETTER

What Did You Think of Thunder 'n' Turf?

Thank you for buying my book! If you enjoyed it, I hope that you could take some time to post a review on your favourite reviews website (where you bought it would be good). Your feedback and support would be really appreciated.

I want you, the reader, to know that your review is very important and so, if you'd like to leave a review, all you have to do is click here and away you go. I wish you all the best in your future success!

Kitty Lucas will return, make sure you don't miss out by subscribing to my newsletter. It comes out once per month and you can join it here:

http://bit.ly/kitty-lucas